An
Imperfect
Spy

ALSO BY AMANDA CROSS

THE THEBAN MYSTERIES
POETIC JUSTICE
DEATH IN A TENURED POSITION*
IN THE LAST ANALYSIS
THE JAMES JOYCE MURDERS*
THE QUESTION OF MAX*
SWEET DEATH, KIND DEATH*
NO WORD FROM WINIFRED*
A TRAP FOR FOOLS*
THE PLAYERS COME AGAIN*

Published by Ballantine Books

An

Imperfect

Spy

AMANDA CROSS

BALLANTINE BOOKS • NEW YORK

To Judith Resnik
and Dennis Curtis

But today, peering calmly into his own heart, Smiley knew that he was unled, and perhaps unleadable; that the only restraints upon him were those of his own reason, and his own humanity.

—JOHN LE CARRÉ
SMILEY'S PEOPLE

❦❦ Prologue

Abruptly he felt inside himself the rising panic of frustration beyond endurance.

—JOHN LE CARRÉ

CALL FOR THE DEAD

The man in the first-class seat in the second row by the window had about decided that there would not be an occupant in the adjoining seat. The flight from London to New York was long, and he was glad not to be burdened with company. He placed his brief-case on the extra seat and sighed gratefully. They were about to shut the doors. And then, at the last minute, a woman entered the plane, smiled apologetically at the flight attendant, and paused at the seat next to his. He removed his briefcase, inwardly cursing his luck, knowing the curse showed on his face.

She was old. Old and heavy. Out of shape, with tousled gray hair that needed combing, and styling before that. If he had to have a female companion for the long flight, why not something young, attractive, and forthcoming, or even not forthcoming? Old women were the devil. They found an excuse to talk to you, they found some question to ask, and then, before you knew it, you were hearing their life story and were in danger of being bored out of your mind, feigning sleep the only release. Really, it was too bad. She was, at least, on the aisle seat; old women had to pee every god-damn minute, and she would have had to step over him, or awake him from sleep, with endless, boring apologies, every other god-

1

damn minute. The flight attendant had asked for her name, as they do in first class to verify one's right to sit there, but he had been unable to make it out.

The woman requested a Bloody Mary and then buckled herself into her seat neatly and without fuss, although she had to stretch the seat belt to its absolute limits to get it around her bulging middle. Then, after extracting a notebook, pen, and book from her briefcase, she stowed it under the seat in front of her and went quietly to work. Unable to contain his curiosity, he strained and glanced until he could read the title of her book; but only the chapter headings topped the pages. The book was, he eventually gathered, on Freud, and she seemed to find it amusing, at times chuckling quietly to herself and making a note. An intellectual, it appeared, a professional, and probably anti-Freudian at that. He was a psychoanalyst, but he was determined that she would never find that out. If she started babbling to him about Freud, he would listen as patiently as possible, and then retreat into his nap. Anyway, he needed to think.

Irritatingly, in light of his carefully contrived defenses, she paid no attention to him. When their meals were served, with cloths and the additional attentions first class offered, she went right on reading, although she had changed her book for a paperback: frivolity with food, he supposed. She was holding her book with the left hand while she ate with her right, and he could see its title easily: John le Carré: *Tinker, Tailor,* something. So she was at heart a lowbrow, after all. Like him she had preferred white wine with her meal; unlike him, she had ordered the beef rather than the fish. He was intensely annoyed to discover that he was observing her with considerably more interest than she was bestowing on him. He disliked old—well, older, as one had to say these days—women; she was almost old enough to be his mother, and he certainly disliked his mother, whom he saw infrequently; in fact, not at all. His training analyst had encouraged him to break off all contact with her. He thought, furthermore, that women ought to keep themselves trim as they aged. How could they expect a man to look at them if they let themselves go that way? Her nails were clipped short and she wore no wedding ring. Probably had never even had any. Lesbian, perhaps; almost certainly, he then decided. This raised his spirits. No wonder she ignored him; ignoring men was the whole point of being a dyke, wasn't it?

After dinner, they showed a movie. With the lights dimmed, she went on reading her le Carré paperback for a while by the single illumination offered from the panel above their chairs. Then she put away her book, stretched out her legs over her briefcase—her legs, unlike his, were not long, permitting her to do this—closed her eyes, and appeared to go to sleep. He realized, as he, too, closed his eyes, that he needed to take a leak, and that he would have to wake her, climb over her (what a thought), and then, when he had done, climb back. He unfastened his seat belt, which he had, unaccountably, left fastened around him; he usually unfastened it even before permission to do so was given by the officious signals. He touched her shoulder, rising as he did so. She stepped into the aisle to let him through; when he returned she was not in her seat, having apparently decided to avail herself simultaneously of the facilities. He thus avoided stepping over her when he returned; immediately he affected sleep, lest her return inspire her to talk. But once she had, upon returning, immediately resumed her slumbers, he decided to follow the movie and dug out the earphones; it was as idiotic as one might expect. He kept glancing at her, unable to prevent himself from doing this. It was exactly, he thought, looking at her in the face of her self-containment, like deciding nothing could induce you to attend a certain party, only to discover you had not been invited. Rejection is never easy. That, perhaps, was why he had, unaccountably, spoken to her near the end of their journey.

The flight attendant had approached them and said that it was the last call for drinks. Would they like some brandy, something like that, some after-dinner drink? He ordered a Courvoisier; she said she would have an aquavit if they had one. She smiled at the attendant. "I took up aquavit in Sweden," she said to him. "Probably you don't carry any aquavit on this flight." But they did. And he

3

found himself, actually found himself, asking to have one, too, instead of his brandy. He had by this time noticed that she wore sneakers, or running shoes, or something inappropriately athletic, and reacted even more unfavorably to that. Yet he ordered her drink. He had no idea why. Except, he had to admit, that he, too, had learned to like aquavit in Scandinavia some years ago. He told her this.

She smiled pleasantly, quickly, but did not answer.

"Are you a professor?" he heard himself asking. She looked like a professor. Damn it, she looked like you had sent to Central Casting for a woman professor: probably no sense of humor, no sense of proportion, didn't know how to play the game. He knew the type; they turned up in medical school and psychoanalytic institutes, too, more's the pity.

"Yes," she said. She was not encouraging him. She did not ask him what he was. She didn't want to know.

"I'm a doctor," he heard himself say, not qualifying the kind.

"I see," she said. And she smiled. She had a rather nice smile, he would give her that. For an old, out-of-shape dame. And he was suddenly embarrassed. She looked full at him as she said "I see," and he could tell she had known exactly what he was thinking all along. She had met his type before. No doubt she was chuckling to herself, behind her double chins. It was maddening.

He refused to say another word. She went back to her book, the hardcover book on Freud this time, and he pretended to consult some papers. He was seething. Yet what, after all, had she done? Nothing except leave him alone. Passive-aggressive, of course. She knew she couldn't get his attention any other way. And he had fallen for it. That was how that kind of woman was; like his mother. They had to put you down, one way or another.

After the plane had landed, she retrieved her clothes bag from the rack up front, and left the plane before him. He saw her hurry up the enclosed walk into the terminal, where she disappeared.

* * *

Nor would he have dreamed of telling a word of this to anyone, if the police hadn't got onto him. They'd traced him through the airline tickets. "But what have I to do with her?" he had asked at first. "We hardly talked; and then she vanished into the terminal."

That was it, it transpired. She had vanished into the terminal and, as far as anyone could discover, out of the world. She hadn't been heard from since.

He felt mildly triumphant hearing this, though he did not say so. He said he had hardly spoken to her; how could he possibly help them? It was only after careful questioning by the two investigators that the whole story emerged. If it was a story. They got it on videotape, as it happened, so there it was, preserved forever. He had, at first, offered a dry account without any of his actual thoughts or angers, but the investigators got the entire narration in the end. Even long afterward, no one who had known her could decide if that had been a triumphant exit for the lady professor or, for her, just a characteristic exchange with that sort of professional man. They inclined, eventually, to the latter. After all, she had walked off into thin air, and no doubt men like this wonderful example had driven her to it. And yet—would she have wanted to give them the satisfaction of just disappearing? For who knew better than a woman professor that disappearing into thin air was what most professional men, given their druthers, would have required of her?

And there, for a time, the matter rested.

One calls it politeness, whereas in fact it is nothing but weakness. . . . Weakness and an inability to live a self-sufficient life independent of institutions . . . and emotional attachments.

—JOHN LE CARRÉ
TINKER, TAILOR, SOLDIER, SPY

When, after many months had passed and Kate Fansler was able calmly to review that frenzied year, it seemed to her portentously coincidental that it had begun with her thinking of le Carré's George Smiley, whose final adventures against his Soviet enemy Karla she had just been reading. A sentence about Smiley had echoed in her mind as she made her reluctant way toward her old school to deliver a lecture. The school's invitation was one to which she had found no suitable words of refusal. It was then she thought of Smiley: "With dismal foreboding, Smiley agreed on a date. After a lifetime of inventing cover stories for every occasion, he still found it impossible to talk his way out of a dinner invitation."

Or an invitation to one's old school, Kate assured him, walking toward the crosstown bus. True, she had not had a lifetime of cover stories, she had kept one name and one identity, but while she had hardened her heart against many social occasions, against dinner parties, cocktail parties, and especially against reunions of any sort, a summons from her own school seemed immediately to lock her into an unwilling, deeply resented acquiescence.

Once on the bus, Kate brooded further. Having passed the statistical point of midlife—assuming greater length of life these days than the Bible's conservative estimate—she had determined not to make policy, to decide on everything as it came along. Policy limited one and discouraged thought. All the same, it might have been said that she had a policy against returning to one's old school or college, a policy the more stringent the more distant the return from one's original attendance. Nonetheless here she was on her way to the Theban, the renowned girls' private school from which she had graduated decades ago.

"Surely you aren't thinking of going back to that place to give a talk!" Reed had said, astonished. Kate could see he was seriously worried, almost as though her going were a symptom of physical or intellectual decadence.

"I couldn't refuse," she had answered, grumbling the inevitable excuse of all those snared into accepting unwelcome invitations. "The headmistress asked me to give one of the talks for high school parents this fall, and pointed out with a certain emphasis that I had refused every invitation to revisit the place since that incident with the dogs so long ago."[1]

"But that was another headmistress," Reed had said. He had always found the elegance of Kate's education daunting.

"Of course it was; I didn't owe that one a favor, as the hideous phrase goes. Rather the other way around. But it was this one I had to plead with twice to get in the brilliant child of a friend, the child having adamantly refused to behave in a way expected of an applicant to the Theban. To be both frank and crude, I rather thought my donations covered my part of the bargain, but of course the Theban never confuses money and service, and of course they shouldn't."

"Couldn't someone else talk to the damn parents?" Reed had not unreasonably asked. They were having their evening drink, and as sometimes happened now when they had both had wearing days,

[1] *The Theban Mysteries*

the talk, although softened by alcohol and intimacy, had an irritable edge.

"I appear to be the only professor available for the job, and everyone has expressed, or is purported to have expressed, an interest in the academic situation of the moment. Aware of all the invective swirling around about the canon, and 'political correctness'— that appalling and meaningless term—the Theban is, as it ever was, anxious to get all the facts and make up its own mind. I clung to the last possible straw by saying that I wasn't exactly impartial in this matter: I did not admire a single thing accomplished in the terrible Republican eighties, and I think the right wing's influence on the country and on public opinion has done terrible damage to us all. Since the Theban always begins by embracing impartiality, I thought that would get me out of the whole thing. Not at all. The Theban, in the person of the current headmistress, was certain I would make my partiality clear, and proceed from there; besides, I suspect they agree with me. Educational funding was horribly cut in the eighties. Still, it is reassuring that such principles of tolerance survive in this world, even if they are but meager sparks."

"But you feel compelled to fan them," Reed said. It wasn't quite a question.

"Oh, who the hell knows?" Kate had peevishly responded, and she felt equally peevish now, recalling the conversation. She had not kept up with any of her classmates from the Theban; time and the pressures of life had taken care of that. What she lacked, unlike those who haunted reunions and exchanged Christmas newsletters, was much curiosity about what had become of her classmates, or how they now looked; certainly she had no wish to learn how many children (grandchildren? Surely not!) they all had. Like all those who had neither borne nor adopted children, Kate found the constant emphasis on progeny tedious and irritating, the more so in that one was not expected to confess such unwomanly indifference.

As the bus entered the transverse Kate tried to divert her thoughts with contemplation of Central Park. Like the Theban, Central Park offered nostalgia, had Kate been inclined that way, which she was not. Some English writer had commented that nostalgia was a "disabling pressure which signifies retreat," and Kate concurred with that wisdom. The park had changed: well, why not? All life changes, but only fools think it has reached its ideal at the exact point where they entered. She stared at the stone walls of the transverse, blackened with soot, at the litter, at the stalled car pulled ineffectually to the side, for the road, serving two-way traffic, consisted of only two lanes with little shoulder room. Above the blackened walls, she could see the Fifty-ninth Street skyline, and the sun glinting off the buildings. Then she was upon the children's zoo. She had never taken a child there, but she had from time to time visited the Central Park Zoo to browse among the seals and the polar bears, and the king penguins, whose parenting habits were described on the signs with frank amazement: the male alone looked after the hatching egg. And then there were the snow monkeys, who had had, one cold winter, to be removed to warmer quarters: they were, it seemed, less suited to American than Japanese urban cold.

Central Park has hills I used to sled on, Kate thought, surrendering to memory and its inevitable resentments, hills now flattened for endless expansion of the Metropolitan Museum, providing them with more galleries than they can guard, therefore more than they can open. And where in Central Park was the Shakespeare garden? Farther uptown, she seemed to remember. She had not visited it since being conducted through it as a child. It was said that every plant mentioned in Shakespeare's plays grew there. Kate, who could scarcely tell a narcissus from a hyacinth, a primrose from a pansy, and had not the faintest idea what chamomile looked like, though she remembered well enough Falstaff's words about it—oh, the hell with Central Park, though in fact Kate loved it still. She did, however, remind herself that Central Park contained only two statues of famous women: Mother Goose and Alice in Wonderland. She supposed one would have to include the new mammoth bear at the playground on East Seventy-ninth Street, female, one supposed, since it sported on each side a cub. Male bears, one understood, went their solitary unencumbered way. And then the bus had come to the end of its route, and the driver opened the doors with a finality that demanded the immediate departure of all within. Kate began the familiar trudge along the avenue to the Theban.

"I must begin," Kate said into the microphone, facing the parents, some alumnae of the faithful sort and, she noted with dismay, what appeared to be the greater part of the upper-school faculty, "by frankly stating that although I shall try fairly to present the arguments on both sides of today's academic debates, I am myself on one side, and do not believe that someone on the other side would speak to you as fairly as I shall try to do, or would deny his or her conviction that that side alone spoke for the good and the true. I hope this makes my impartiality clear."

That said, Kate proceeded with her speech. It was not long, and was greeted with more than polite applause and enthusiasm. Many came to speak to her afterward, including members of the faculty, all in Kate's saturnine view astonishingly young. Kate refused the punch offered at the reception following and, when asked if she would like anything else, requested a glass of soda water. Kate was handed this by the headmistress, and was only at the last minute able to prevent herself from exclaiming as she tasted it. For the drink was vodka and tonic, complete with a slice of lime, visually quite indistinguishable from plain soda water. Kate discreetly smiled her gratitude, and bent herself to the mannerly parent waiting to talk to her.

It was only when the event appeared to be drawing to a close, and those at the reception were dispersing, that Kate was confronted by a woman older than most of the audience. She had that air, common to a small percent of Theban graduates, of having since the age of ten thought fashion and beauty aids too boring for words and of having found no reason, in the intervening years, to change her mind. Only the woman's speech betrayed her highly educated status.

Kate and the woman withdrew into an uninhabited corner, and Kate prepared herself for the usual memories of an earlier and, by definition, better time, an agreement that often oddly accompanied praise for Kate's remarks, as though the listener had altogether failed to take in their hardly conservative import. But this woman, it became immediately clear, agreed with what Kate had said because she had heard it.

"Might we talk somewhere away from the madding crowd?" the woman said. Oh, God, Kate thought, but fortified with her vodka, she felt generous enough to spare a little time. "Let's try to find a spare classroom," she said.

They mounted the stairs and Kate walked purposefully into the first classroom they came to; it was designed for younger children. Never inclined to perch on tiny chairs, Kate sat on a desk, put her drink and bag down beside her, and tried to look simultaneously interested and without much time to spare.

"Just to prove to you how attentive I am," the woman said, "I observe that what you are drinking is probably vodka, or maybe gin, and tonic. Could you spare a sip?"

Grinning, Kate handed over her drink. The woman tasted it, smacked her lips in a comical and approving manner, grinned back, and returned the glass.

"Your secret is safe with me," she said. "And," she added, looking around, "I can certainly understand the need for alcoholic resuscitation in this place."

"Did you go to the Theban?" Kate asked.

"Alas, no. Fine education, no doubt, but a little too ladylike for my tastes, or so I guess."

Kate glanced around at the room, at the childish drawings and the admonitions on the blackboard, and found both deeply uninteresting. Probably she should have settled for the corner downstairs; still, one could always claim discomfort and depart.

"If you didn't go to the Theban," Kate remarked, "may I ask what you were doing here? You have a daughter or granddaughter who attended the school?"

12

"Alas, not even that excuse. I am quite without child dependents, quite fancy-free, another definition of widowhood and advancing age. I came for the express purpose of meeting you."

"And what purpose had you in meeting me?" Kate asked, putting down her now empty glass.

"Shall I get you another?" the older woman asked. "I could manage, you know, no doubt about that."

"No, thank you. Your purpose?"

"We are about to be colleagues, in a manner of speaking."

Kate hoped she did not look as astonished as she felt. Her department's hiring a woman of that age and, well, nonconformity and frankness, hardly seemed possible.

The woman seemed to read her mind. "Not at your exalted institution," she said. "At the Schuyler Law School. You are teaching there next semester, are you not?"

Kate stared. "I've only just decided," she said. "Not two days ago. I haven't even yet met the man I'm teaching with. How did you know?"

"Because I'm head of the secretarial room at the Schuyler and I know everything. Your husband's running a clinic. Damn good idea. Schuyler's never had a real clinic before, only simulated ones. Not without their uses, but they don't really help people, do they? Well, I thought I'd say hello, greetings, and good luck at putting some life into that antediluvian institution."

"Thank you," Kate said faintly, no other response occurring to her.

"I've learned a certain amount about you," the woman said, stretching her legs before her as she perched comfortably on a tiny chair. "You're less a lady than your mother, or her mother, and so on back through the generations. I've no doubt of that. You haven't got children, you don't indulge in social rituals, and you take personal and professional risks. But the risks are all within the confines of the acceptable. Just outside those confines are a lot of folks who don't play by any rules you would recognize, let alone condone. You have a job with tenure; there's no way they can take it away from you, however much they would like to. Sure, they can make your life unpleasant, I suppose, but financially you're safe, and if my investigation is even approximate, you'd be safe financially if the whole university went up in smoke. Don't get me wrong. You use your money in the best possible ways, you fight for the right things. You didn't take your husband's name. You try to help the innocent and those in trouble. But you have, I suspect, never dealt for any length of time either with the dispossessed or the desperately frightened. Not that you're worse than anyone else from the same background. In fact, you're much better, which is why I seek your acquaintance."

Kate looked at the woman as though she feared her drink had contained not vodka but some hallucinogenic drug that the woman had been willing to share because she had developed a tolerance for it. Pull yourself together, Kate, she admonished herself. Her back was already signaling less than absolute delight with its position on the child-sized desk, and if she wasn't drugged, she was certainly cornered by a fanatic.

"I hope I haven't offended you. I do admire you; I hope that's clear."

"You haven't offended me," Kate said, "though I can't guess"—she was suddenly overcome with irritation and pushed herself from the desk onto her feet—"why we're having this conversation, even if you do work in the secretarial room of the Schuyler Law School. I'm sure you're right about me, though I can't imagine how you found all that out, let alone why you wanted to. As to my life, I console myself with the thought that we must all work where we are, do what we can. I don't cross over the edge, but I stay as close to it as I can without falling apart and doing no good whatever. Perhaps," she added, "that's all just self-justification." But why do I keep answering her? Kate wondered.

"Thank you for that," the woman said. "I've crossed over the edge, and nothing learned at the Theban or afterward would have enabled anyone to do that. If you understand that, you understand a good deal."

14

"I understand nothing," Kate said. "I've finished my drink, and these damn desks are in no way appropriate to the mature physique." She rubbed her back. "Might we get to the point of how I can help you?"

"I don't need your help," the woman said. "I just thought we might meet. I wanted to get a line on you, if truth be told. Well, bye-bye."

And with a comically girlish wave, she walked out of the room, leaving Kate staring after her in wonder.

"I don't get it," was Reed's comment after Kate had arrived home demanding that he listen to her day's adventures rather more urgently than usual. He hardly commented on her lecture at the Theban, on which she had not, in any case, lingered, but had followed with rather more attention her conversation with the nameless woman. "I can't imagine what she wanted from you, or why you even listened to her," he said, somewhat testily, and they went on to talk of other things.

"It's a funny thing," Reed said later that night when he was undressing. He paused with his hands on his belt. "Nobody ever wanders into my office or my lectures the way they do with you, demanding acquaintance and conversation in the most amazing circumstances."

"That's because I, unlike you, am an amateur detective with a reputation to be envied," Kate answered. They were both feeling much better.

On the following Sunday morning, Reed was cooking bacon in a frying pan when Kate joined him. She stood in the kitchen doorway regarding him: tall, frowning, his glasses fogging slightly as he concentrated on turning the pieces of bacon and separating them in the pan. She found him, at that moment, utterly endearing. She chuckled.

"I know, I know," he said, smiling. "I ought to do them in the broiler, but there are some ways in which I prefer to stick to the simpler, more primitive methods."

Kate perched on a high stool they kept in the kitchen for just such moments. It was a large kitchen, and she had often thought of furnishing it with an easy chair, but somehow had never got around to it.

"It's not the way you cook bacon, of which I highly approve," she said. "I was thinking about descriptions of rooms in books I've read, current novels. No one can enter a room anymore, even to murder or interrogate the occupant, without first describing every detail. I think it's a new form of literary madness. Imagine me in a novel entering this room to find you cooking bacon."

"Okay," Reed said, "do you want just bacon and toast, by the way, or bacon and eggs? How uncommitted to a health regimen are you feeling?"

"Utterly uncommitted," Kate said.

"Good. Go on with your description."

Kate wriggled herself more firmly onto the stool and sipped the Bloody Mary he had made for each of them. Their Sunday brunch libation, they called it. "Here goes," she said. "First of all, I would describe *you.* 'She saw a distinguished face, with warm brown eyes gazing behind his glasses from a height which suggested he did not have to strain to see and understand it all'—that sort of thing. 'Strong brows, an air of sexuality'—you know. Having described you, I go on to the kitchen. 'A room of generous dimensions, perhaps twenty feet square, obviously the scene of many intimate conversations and meals.' "

"If you're describing this kitchen," Reed said, "you're bonkers. It's nowhere near twenty feet square—closer to fifteen, and not square by a long shot. I shall overlook," he added, turning bacon strips, "my strong brows and sexual exudations."

"Is there such a word as *exudations*? I've scarcely begun. Remember, there is a plot here, for which we are supposedly reading. 'The north side of the room was the utility side, equipped with a superior range, a board on which hung many gleaming copper pots, a large sink with a drain board—' "

"Kate," Reed said, "I get the picture. Is there a plot?"

"I don't know; it is probably a quite awful plot. Shall I go on?"

"No. I am frowning with my strong brows and exuding irritation. Do you want your eggs turned over?"

"Definitely. But let me describe the old-fashioned stove at which you are working, with a look of gentle concentration on your manly features. . . ."

Reed, who was frying eggs in butter, picked up the pan and made throwing gestures. He had placed his bacon slices on a plate covered with paper towels.

"All right, all right," Kate said. "I'm starved, as a matter of fact. No toast?" she added, looking around.

"Damn," Reed said. "You and your descriptions." He got up to fetch the toast.

Kate threw him a kiss as they began eating.

"All right," he said when they had finished. "What is it; what the hell is it, Kate?"

"I'm going through a phase."

"What?"

"My mother used to say that when I was being difficult. 'Kate's going through a phase.' "

"And were you? Are you?"

"I rather think I am."

Reed snorted. "This is beginning to sound like the dialogue in a Robert Parker novel. Not as clever, of course, but short and snappy."

"He certainly doesn't go in for descriptions, except of what the male characters are wearing. He always tells you what he's wearing, Spenser that is—"

"What phase?"

"Let's call it a midlife crisis."

"Let's not," Reed said. "I've always scorned that phrase. Of course people have crises all through life, people who think, that is, but those that happen in midlife, which is most of life, cannot be identified by so simple a phrase." He smiled at her. "I know one can get tired of teaching *Middlemarch* for the hundredth time. I'm not sure I could manage to read it for the second time with any equanimity. That's one of the costs of teaching, isn't it? One has to listen over and over again to one's students discovering what one has long ago mastered. But if one doesn't want to do that, why teach? There are other ways to pass a life."

"It's not exactly *Middlemarch*," Kate said. "It's not the literature, really. It's not even the students, although that comes closer to the problem. I mean, was ever a generation, even a generation of those interested enough to enter graduate school, so abysmally unprepared, uninformed, unknowledgeable? And don't tell me I sound like a right-wing defender of the canon or I'll kill you. The students know many things I don't; I'd like to learn what they know. But it comes over me in waves that sitting around discussing *Middlemarch* —which Virginia Woolf called the last novel written for adults—is not going to lead them or me to any common ground. And I will not join the right wing, whose views I was attacking only the other afternoon at the Theban, because between them and the ignorant, improperly motivated kids, I'll take the kids hands down."

"Finished?" Reed asked.

"Yes," Kate said. "Sorry to be boring you; sorry to be ranting at you. We used to understand each other. Now the best we can achieve is a rather attenuated tolerance. Do you know what Adrienne Rich said to a friend? 'We're unable to write love, as we so much wish to do, without writing politics.' The same is true of talking, I suspect. Let's face it, Reed, you used to find my animadversions entertaining, if not persuasive. Whatever we've had, we've lost it, just the way my classes have."

"We seem to have gone from higher education to our marriage with amazing haste."

"We did," Kate said, "and it's no good looking all innocence. If you hadn't said *finished?* in that supercilious way, I wouldn't have gone on to marriage. After all, we are married, and you did say it."

"I apologize. Abjectly. What I meant to observe was that you were using your usual decoy methods, running on about one problem when it is, really, only part of the whole. I meant: can't we go on to what's *really* bothering you?"

"If I knew, I'd tell you, honest. Any suggestions?"

"You're acting, if you want to know, like someone who's having an affair."

Kate stared at him. "What you mean," she said, "is that I'm acting like someone who no longer feels quite as happily—no, let's say naturally—married. Furthermore," she added, before he could say anything, "the problem's probably mine. I'm restless and feeling at an end but not at a beginning. It hasn't really to do with us at all."

Which was a brave speech, Kate thought to herself. The truth was, she was a lot closer to having an affair than she liked to admit, even to herself. She was, in fact, having a pleasant and somehow reassuring dalliance with a younger colleague; they began by having lunch, then afternoon drinks, and then, ultimately, a more passionate if unconsummated interlude in his apartment while his wife was away. Kate, who had met the wife, felt lousy about the whole thing and did not go again to his apartment: there had been some talk of a hotel. No doubt it would go on like that indefinitely. Kate had "wandered" on a few other occasions, and found little significance in those actions. She had never discussed it with Reed, and did not intend to do so now. Like a character in a story by Sylvia Townsend Warner, Kate thought constancy the important element in a relationship, fidelity less so. Kate had been fond of many men; from time to time these friendships had led to an "affair." Always, the sex had flavored but had not embodied the friendship, which in almost all cases continued beyond passion. That was, Kate understood, and suspected Reed understood, the way she was.

What troubled her now was not the possibility of an affair, or even Reed's reference to it. His remark was most uncharacteristic of their alliance, and boded no good, but that was not really the problem either. The problem was that something had gone oddly wrong with their marriage, and this possible affair, accomplished or not, was, unlike any other, overdetermined by causes more serious than restlessness, opportunity, or mutual affection.

"Let's call it a period of dryness," Kate offered for something to say. "I seem to get it the way others get hay fever."

"In what way has it to do with us, with me?" Reed asked. And suddenly Kate felt a surge of love for him, his honesty, his reasonableness: the fact that he cared rather than wanted to argue about it. Oddly, though not that oddly in a marriage essentially strong, she suddenly recognized something of the problem and could name it.

"When I met you, and learned to love you," Kate said, "you were a district attorney. Of course you complained constantly about the job, the lack of resources, incompetent young lawyers, the police and the constraints upon them, everything. But you were involved, you seemed excited about some cases."

"And now I'm just a professor of law."

Kate nodded. "It sounds foolish, I know, and outrageous coming from a professor of English literature. But you don't seem as alive to me as you used to. Something's gone out of you, Reed. You're just as dear, but the electricity's gone."

"But I'm starting a clinic at a law school that's never had one, not a nonsimulated one, at least," Reed said. "And you're going to teach there, so we'll have the experience of discovering a new institution together. Do you want more than that? I'll quit teaching law altogether if you want. I'll take extra-early retirement. I'll stay on leave an extra year. What can I do to make the electricity come back?" He took off his glasses and wiped them. Kate was shocked to realize how moved he was. She reached her hand out to him, across the table.

"You're right, of course," he said. "I haven't wanted to face it. Everyone keeps complaining about what's wrong with higher education in this country, though I admit they don't tend to concentrate on law schools. But the trouble is, professors can tire of teaching; they need adventure. I suppose that's why they get sabbaticals, and not just to write books, as is supposed. That's why they keep wandering off to conferences in strange cities. You want adventure. I want it, too, which is why I've agreed to do this clinic. But the truth is, my dear Kate, marrying you and living with you was, or so it seemed to me, all the adventure that I needed."

"That is the most generous and the kindest statement I have ever heard from man or beast," Kate said. She suddenly felt better. "Of course you mustn't think of doing anything rash. We have to work out, and you have especially to work out, what change, if any, you want. Meanwhile, there's the Schuyler Law School. I may even discover how one teaches law and literature at the same time. And you'll be doing something important. Let's be glad of that."

Reed came over to her side of the table and pulled her to her feet. He held her as though they were about to begin ballroom dancing. "I don't think it's just my job, or even just our marriage," he said. "But, after all, what do you know about law schools, anyway? You need an informed consultant, and one in addition to your teaching companion; we shall have a new adventure together. Kate, my love, everyone intelligent and sensitive, and you're those as much as anyone on earth, has times when the old is worthless and the new unimaginable. Anyway, you are inclined to periods of downness and a sense of futility; as you said, it's happened before. Please, let's try to get through this. There may be casual excitements available, and you may feel inclined to them, but let's not lose what we have."

"Someone once told me you're too good to be believed."

"I'm not good; in fact, at the moment I'm angry and close to madness, if you want to know. I just happen to love you, so I'm trying to be reasonable when I don't feel the least fucking bit reasonable. If you want to know, I feel like hell."

"So do I," Kate said. "So do I. But much better for the bacon and eggs. We shall grow old together, Reed, our arteries hardening at an equally rapid pace."

"But not our ideas, our minds, our hearts, or so I hope," Reed said. "Or so I hope."

2

*"If I regret anything at all, it's the way we
wasted our time and skills. All the false alleys, and
bogus friends, the misapplication of our energies.
All the delusions we had about who we were."*

—JOHN LE CARRÉ
THE SECRET PILGRIM

Several evenings later a rather frightening thing happened. They
had gone out to dinner, during which they again had one of their
desultory conversations. Kate had observed: "I think we overestimate the importance of sex." Reed had looked at her warily. She
had been given lately to such pronouncements, and this time, as
usual, his face had reflected his unsureness of how to respond.

"I don't really mean sex," Kate had not too clearly continued. "I
mean sex as a substitute for whatever else is wrong; and, I suspect,
in the case when something else is wrong, only friendship counts.
And the only reason friendship counts is because we can use conversation to discover our lives."

"Pretend I'm a friend. Pretend we've only just met, and you've
decided to consult me because I have an understanding face."

"You do have an understanding face, and I haven't the slightest
idea what I'm talking about, so your understanding face will get us
nowhere. I guess I mean I don't really care about sex or what comes
of it, I don't even think about it. It's just a way to stop thinking
about other things. The general sense of discontent. You know."

Reed smiled. "My students always say *you know*, when it's perfectly clear that I don't know and am doubtful whether they do either."

"In this case," Kate said, "you *know*. I'm saying it isn't about you, and there isn't really anything else. It's just me. The hell with me. Tell me about law clinics, about the one you're starting at Schuyler Law."

Reed looked at her for a long moment and then complied. "Well, as we were saying the other day, the chance to do a clinic at Schuyler Law came at just the right time. Blair Whitson, a young law professor there, the one whom you're going to teach the law and literature course with, seems to have become something of a minor revolutionary, which he wasn't when we first met. Anyway, when he suggested that I start a clinic at the school, it seemed a welcome change. I'd recently gone to my dean and others, people at my law school in charge of such things, to try to start a clinic, a prison project, perhaps connected to a project for battered women, but they were a bit too Ivy League to be willing to support it, or maybe they just didn't want another clinic, or maybe they didn't want a regular faculty, nonclinic person, starting a clinic. Anyway, they turned me down. So this Schuyler offer was doubly welcome: help a friend and have a new adventure; sounds like an ad."

Kate smiled encouragingly.

"I've thus decided," Reed continued, "that Schuyler Law School shall have a clinic, helping those once convicted but who have some real reason to believe that their convictions were improperly obtained or that their sentences are illegal in some way, or who have stories of mistreatment by prison staff. There are even those who are improperly in prison, or at least believe they are."

"Why improperly?" Kate asked.

"Many reasons. Sometimes it's a case of noncitizens having served their term and being held because they are illegal immigrants who can't be deported because their home countries won't take them. Then there are all the women who need help, some of whom have killed battering husbands, either before the battered woman syndrome became accepted, or whose lawyers had never heard of it."

"It certainly sounds nobler than teaching law and literature together. Whatever made your friend Blair think that might be a good idea?"

"First, I persuaded him, because when you're on leave you do much better, I've noticed, if you have some regular, not too demanding, commitment. And persuading him wasn't too hard. Many schools have taken up law and literature courses, and besides, you'll find it interesting. Different points of view. When are you going to talk to Blair about it?"

"Any day now," Kate said. "I've left a message on his machine and he's left one on mine. Reed, not to put too fine a point on it, do you think there's something odd in the fact that we are both going to spend our sabbaticals working at the worst law school in New York and perhaps the whole United States?"

"It isn't the worst law school in the United States, even if it isn't the sort we admire. Many of the students in law schools like Schuyler are older students, returnees, men and women, mostly women, who have decided they don't want to continue the life they're leading and want to become lawyers. Often the students are very interested, very earnest, and very motivated. Don't be a bloody snob, my dear."

When, later, they returned to their apartment, well fed and considerably more cheerful than they had been, separately or together, for quite a while, still chatting as Reed unlocked the door, they were both flabbergasted into immobility at the sight of an old woman calmly sitting in their foyer, knitting away on a long, woolly creation.

Reed instinctively (as Kate accused him later) moved cautiously forward so that Kate was directly behind him. But Kate had recovered from the adrenaline surge which, having inspired neither fright nor flight, as was its wont, left as suddenly as it had come.

"It's the woman at the Theban I told you about," Kate said.

"How in hell did you get in here?" Reed asked, abandoning his usual civility; she had given him a bad shock.

"Easy," the woman said. "I like to prove that I can rob apartment buildings."

"Why?"

"Why what?"

"Why do you want to prove that?"

"To demonstrate that I'm invisible, of course. That's the whole point, you see. As an oldish woman, I'm invisible and can go anywhere, like someone in a fairy story."

"Ah," Reed said. "So tonight you became invisible and melted through the door like ghosts in movies. You're not a ghost, are you?"

"Almost. This time I didn't play on invisibility, but on conventionality. I simultaneously convinced your doorman that I was harmless, in need of rest, and your aunt." This last was directed at Reed.

"You aren't old enough to be my aunt," Reed said inconsequentially. Kate had already noted after one meeting that one tended to be inconsequential when conversing with this woman.

"Ours was a large family of which I was the youngest, your father the oldest. I didn't, as I explained to him, get to New York often, and perhaps you hadn't got the message I left on your machine about my altered time of arrival. I was also feeling faint."

"My father?" Reed asked.

"Well, I said my name was Amhearst, so it had to be your father. I shan't presume upon the relationship; please don't be concerned. I just wanted to demonstrate my thesis and my ability. I was counting, of course, on the fact that you were unlikely to have discussed your extended family with the doorman. That took a certain amount of perspicacity also; give me credit."

Reed pulled himself together. "Do come in," he said. "But please, don't do that to me again. It won't be a trick, for one thing, now that the doorman considers you my aunt."

"Point taken," the woman said.

They moved into the living room, where Kate offered the woman a drink. She chose a single-malt scotch, in which they joined her, and settled herself into a chair.

"I had another reason for wanting to see you," the woman said, "apart from proving my skills. This is really excellent whisky," she added, gently smacking her lips as she had done after her sip of Kate's drink at the Theban. "I thought the time had come to admit to you that I wasn't altogether honest about my position at Schuyler."

Reed and Kate continued to regard her steadily, as though she might vanish if not held constantly in their gaze.

"I have the job illegally. That is, I can do what I told them I can do, and I do it very well, but I'm not who they think I am. I borrowed the credentials from someone else, Social Security number, résumé, the lot. She's retreated to Nova Scotia and couldn't care less. If they find out, I'll say I stole everything. If they don't—and I shall take jolly good care that they won't—she'll have a bit more Social Security than she might otherwise have had. Her name's Harriet Furst, and that's the name I use. Please call me Harriet."

"But you do run the secretarial room at Schuyler Law School?" Kate spoke as one peering through a fog.

"Oh, dear, yes, and very well, too, if I may say so. If you have a little more of that excellent whisky, and don't mind staying up awhile, I'll tell you the truth about myself. Not all the truth, but as much as I dare, and I dare the more as I grow older. Montaigne."

Reed poured her more single-malt scotch, and sat back as though, like the wedding guest, he had been stopped and mesmerized by the Ancient Mariner.

Harriet sipped her drink appreciatively. "Have you ever seen a catalpa tree drop its leaves?" she asked.

Kate shook her head, while Reed continued in his mesmerized state. "I don't even think I've seen a catalpa tree *with* its leaves," Kate added, for something to say. The question was unusual, but then, everything about Harriet was unusual.

"They drop them all at once—*boom*, like that—while you're

watching. People have often talked about seeing the last leaf fall from a tree, but that's nothing, believe me, to the sight of a catalpa tree deciding winter has come.

"Well, that's how it was with me. *Boom.* All the leaves fell off, and so instead of bowing out gracefully and slowly, as one is supposed to do, I just decided to disappear. Like the catalpa leaves— all at once. No backward glances, no regrets, and no chance to hear from anyone. It was John le Carré who gave me the idea. One simply decides to become a spy. We're all spies, of course, but some more than others.

"By the way," she said to Kate, "I know more about you than I let on at the Theban. I know you smoke—at least from time to time, though you're trying to give it up—which is good news, because so do I. Do you mind if I smoke now; would you like one?" she said to Kate. Kate shook her head. "Too bad," Harriet said. "I'm at the age where pleasure counts for more than safety; I'm only interested in a few more intense years anyway. I heard you also drink, imbibe caffeine, and consider animal fat essential to human endurance. That's why I decided I'd be glad to meet you, even though I'd decided I'd have to meet you even if I wasn't glad; but I'm glad I was glad."

Kate nodded. She thought of saying "I'm glad, too," and then decided she wasn't sure she was.

"I've disappeared," Harriet continued. "Vanished, unable to be found, gone. Registered as a missing person, but not likely to make it off the back list. I figured if le Carré's characters could just disappear, melt into the scene, remain unnoticed, so could I. Did you read *The Russia House*? The Smiley books are the best, but once Alec Guinness played Smiley, he didn't seem to belong to le Carré anymore. Understandable of course. In le Carré's books chaps just disappear, sometimes twice. I decided to disappear, too. I'm a big le Carré fan; I know he's a lost cause when it comes to women, but at least he's not Norman Mailer. Anyway, I decided to become a spy. Oh, not for government; crooks and bastards, the lot of them.

But a modern spy. And I decided to spy at the Schuyler Law School."

"Why did you decide to be a spy at all?" Kate asked.

"Because I thought I'd be damn good at it. There's nothing like an old woman to bypass anyone, even doormen standing right in front of those signs that say 'All visitors must be announced.' You have a well-run building, so I had to pretend to be an aunt. Usually, they just assume I live there, since plenty of old women live there or visit regularly, and we all look alike. It works like a charm. I don't know why I didn't think of it years ago."

"What did you do before you disappeared?" Kate asked. "Before all the leaves fell off simultaneously?" Reed seemed distinctly stunned, and Kate felt it incumbent upon her to keep up the conversation. Besides, she found to her surprise that she really wanted to know.

"I was a professor, of course. What else? In a university outside Boston, even beyond Cambridge. I had a house like everybody else, with a dog, and a yard with plenty of space for a garden. I rather thought I'd take up gardening one day, when I had the time. Sheer rot, of course. Like all those people who tell you they want time to read all the books they've never got to. If they had wanted to read, they would have read. And I would have gardened. One day I realized that I would never plant a flower, not so much as a bulb, and that I would never go back to my office again and listen to all those second-rate men and women without enough guts to face up to a belligerent mouse. So I just took off for London over the Christmas holidays, having sold my house to a friend who had always admired it but couldn't afford its real worth and who was willing to take on the dog into the bargain, came back, and just disappeared. I assumed that they would assume that I wouldn't have sold my house if I wasn't planning to die, and such plans could easily be understood in the light of my cantankerous nature, which had recently become more so. I vanished, presumed dead, though not legally of course. But legally doesn't mean a thing to me."

"But—" Kate said, and stopped.

"I know all the questions," Harriet said, "so why don't I answer the ones I can think of, and that will leave you fewer to ponder. But don't hold back. Ask what you want, when you want. Just don't tell anyone you know me, have met me, or have heard a single thing about me, not so much as a whisper. Agreed?"

Kate nodded. This new mode of listening to someone who talked more than she did and did not expect her to talk at all was, she found, refreshing and remarkably little effort. Reed, nudged by Kate, nodded, too.

"I had already cashed in my pension; fortunately, my university lets you do that after sixty. My husband had a pension, and I had persuaded him to take bigger benefits for his lifetime, not survivor benefits. He died five years ago, and managed to enjoy his retirement without ever stooping to gardening or reading Tolstoy or anything he regretted not having read before. Actually, he became enthralled with computers, but that doesn't really have anything to do with this story. If there's a computer heaven, he's in it. I turned the money I got for my house into cash, and decided, since I had disappeared and wanted to be presumed dead, that I would move into the cash economy, which is bigger than any of us who get paid by salary checks have ever supposed. It's not all that hard. I get paid by check at the Schuyler, of course, and I cash it at the bank where I've opened an account with my nice phony identification, but apart from my Schuyler check I live strictly on a cash basis. I rent a room for cash, I pay cash for everything. I'm an underground spy in America, taking all my cues from le Carré. Fun. And," she added, "as I said, Harriet is a new name for a new incarnation, so don't waste your time going through academic catalogs."

"Why did you want to meet me because I was going to teach at Schuyler Law School?" Kate asked.

"You know, it does show that things do sometimes change under pressure," Harriet said. "There's been so much flack at dear old Schuyler Law about anti-woman and -minority attitudes that they've agreed to have a course in women in literature and the law, to be taught by a law professor and someone from outside the law, who will, it is to be hoped, lead the discussion off into byways concerning Jane Eyre, the wills in *Wuthering Heights*, and the trials of Orestes and Billy Budd. Yes, my dear. I know, I haven't answered your question about the Theban. I had to appear to meet you accidentally; surely you see that."

"No," Kate said. "I don't. Why did you have to meet me accidentally?"

"Well, you had to have met me before I broke into your apartment; you recognized me, don't you see? I had to talk to you, but I had to do it privately, and I had to establish myself so that you would talk to me privately. As you are. I don't blame you for feeling you met a pussycat who turned into a tiger," Harriet said. "I feel the same myself."

Reed had decided that the moment for him to enter this conversation, if it could be called a conversation, had arrived. "What I don't understand," he said, "and I don't think Kate does either, is why you had to see her, privately or otherwise. True, you will both be working at the Schuyler Law School, as will I. But if you wanted to make our acquaintance, surely there were less dramatic ways to do it."

Harriet stared at her empty glass, twirling it around. "Do you remember," she asked, "that woman faculty member from Schuyler Law, just recently tenured, who died subsequently as the result of falling beneath a truck?"

"Vaguely," Reed said. It was now Kate's turn to disappear into a profound silence. "I have only the faintest memory of the woman's death. In fact, it wouldn't have received much attention in this violent city if they hadn't decided at Schuyler Law to mock her by publishing a parody of her ideas after her death."

"Disaster hardly grabs our attention in this city, dearly as I love it," Harriet said. "The point is, did she fall or was she pushed? Under the truck, I mean. The police found no evidence of her being pushed, but that doesn't mean she wasn't. Doesn't it strike either of you as odd that the first woman faculty they hired met a violent death? Is that too difficult a question? It's the sort of thing I wanted to discuss privately with you two." She looked at Reed.

"It's certainly too difficult a question for tonight," he said. "I've clean run out of energy. We'll reconvene soon, I promise."

"All right then," Harriet said, regarding with a certain plaintiveness her empty glass. "If you say so." She rose to her feet, putting the glass down. "You're angry about my getting in here. That was showing off; I apologize. But please try to trust me. Do you know what Smiley said to the students at Sarratt when they asked him how to recognize a lie? He said: 'Oh, there's *some* art to faulting the liar, of course there is. But the real art lies in recognizing the truth, which is a great deal harder.' " This time she looked at Kate, who shook her head to indicate that Smiley's words were new to her.

"Well," Reed said, "if you two are going to exchange quotations, I'm off to bed. I really do think we've carried on long enough for one evening, don't you?"

"Right you are," Harriet said. "I'm going, and if I come again, it will be because I'm invited and announced nicely by the watchdog downstairs."

And with that they saw her to the door.

🦌🦌 3

"It's time you handed on your wisdom to the new boys, Ned," he had told me over a suspiciously good lunch at the Connaught. "And to the new girls," he added, with a loathsome smirk. "They'll be letting them into the Church next, I suppose."

—JOHN LE CARRÉ
THE SECRET PILGRIM

The next morning, when Kate had got herself up, fed, and ready to face the day, she found a message on her answering machine from Blair Whitson, who reminded her that he was the one who was going to teach the course with her at Schuyler Law and added that he was eager to meet with her. How about lunch today at the Oak Room of the Plaza? He gave his number.

Kate called it, getting his message machine. Kate had got quite used to this exchange of machines, and even thought there was a good deal to be said for it; it allowed tedious arrangements to be made without superfluous interchange or chat, and if one screened calls, it gave one some control over whom one talked to, and when. Also, at least for Kate, the fact remained that if you had something serious to say to a person, it was better said across a table in a pleasant restaurant or, at any rate, face-to-face rather than over the telephone. Machine messages thus happily tended to postpone conversations to the place of meeting. She left a message on Blair Whitson's machine to say she never went out to lunch, but how about dinner tonight in the Oak Room? If yes, say when. If no, say when and where. Reed was going to be busy all evening, and the Oak Room at the Plaza always pleasantly revived in Kate the change from the years when they wouldn't let women in to dine with the men. One needed to assure oneself from time to time that some things do change and, more important these days, stay changed.

She went off to a faculty meeting that she felt required to attend even though she was on leave, and returned to find the completion of arrangements mechanically recorded: 7:30 tonight at the Oak Room. He would recognize her. How? Kate wondered. The table was reserved in his name, should he be delayed.

He was not delayed.

He was at the table when she arrived, stood to greet her, helped her to seat herself, and asked what she wanted to drink. Then he sat down, and Kate reflected that he was certainly the most improbable male revolutionary she had ever encountered. But then, Reed had said he had only recently become a revolutionary; all he wanted, after all, was a real clinic and a law and literature course. Perhaps at Schuyler, at least as Harriet saw it, that was sufficient to qualify one as a revolutionary.

Blair in fact looked, if one had to resort to typecasting, like an admiral who had reached the pinnacle of his profession young. No, she thought, rather like the captain of a ship plying northern seas in the kind of films they used to make about World War II.

Kate lowered her eyes and sipped her drink. A most unfeminist question and unfeminist thoughts: was she really wondering why a man that, well, that *manly*, should be worried about literature and the law, let alone women and the law? One day she would ask him. Looks, after all, she reminded herself sternly, told one little of significance.

"I came to law rather late," he said, as though he had read her mind. "Before that I did nothing but 'mess about with boats.' Isn't that a literary quotation of some sort?"

"*The Wind in the Willows*, I think. Ratty perhaps. Mole was the one with windfalls from aunts. That's *my* favorite phrase."

"It's wonderful to have a literary mind. Anyhow, one day I decided, if I'm going to help fix up the mess in this country, I better stop messing with boats and learn the law. Or maybe I tired of the naval hierarchy and decided to explore the legal hierarchy instead. So here we are, discussing how we can do a little to revive the faculty of the Schuyler Law School. They're so far entrenched in old ways of thinking, and so self-satisfied in their entrenchment, that I don't put it past them to think that those who bother them, or want to change their golden ways, should be snuffed out. That is, if ridicule and nastiness have failed. Cheers."

"Cheers," Kate answered. "Would you mind telling me how you were able to recognize me?"

"No problem. So nice to be able to use that phrase, since so often there *is* a problem. I went to hear my old pal Reed Amhearst lecture on one of the newest wrinkles in criminal law; you were pointed out to me afterward as his lit-crit wife; you had come to hear him. I remembered that when I had to think of a literary type to help me teach this course. I thought, you see, you might be more amenable to adventures in legal realms because of your husband. And then with him doing the clinic, I thought we might as well take up nepotism as well as revolution. Would you like another drink or shall we order?"

"Let's order, by all means," Kate said, feeling rather breathless. First it had been Harriet, now Blair. Reed was going to do a clinic for them while she was teaching a course, and so far everyone they'd met had been surprising. Was that a good sign?

When they had ordered, Kate sat there, feeling somehow the pawn of destiny, and admiring his hair, straight, with some gray beginning, and lying thick like an animal's pelt; his vivid blue eyes, blue, no doubt, from staring at the sea, looked at her, smiling. You'll be writing romantic fiction next, she told herself.

Without waiting for their food to arrive, Blair Whitson apologized for launching into the topic of their proposed course immediately, and then launched. "The fact is," he said, "if we're going to do this course, we've got to start planning yesterday. Sorry to pressure you, but isn't life, at least academic life, always that way? First it's don't do today what you can put off to tomorrow, and then it's hurry up, this stuff was needed yesterday. I'm sure you understand what I mean. I know, I know," he added before Kate could respond, although for once she was thinking and hadn't got yet to a response, "I'm pushing you. Of course I am. The class starts late next week. We can muddle through the first meeting with reading lists and gab about papers, participation, the usual. But after that, of course, we're going to have to say something both literary and legal."

"Simultaneously?" Kate asked. She leaned back in her chair and took in the scene. The Oak Room at the Plaza, when you got right down to it, was an odd place to plan a revolution, or even a course on literature and law. For some idiotic reason, Kate thought of a story she had heard about Marlene Dietrich arriving in some elegant dining place just like this wearing white tie and tails. "We do not allow women in trousers," the maître d' had proclaimed. With which Dietrich took off the trousers and tossed them aside. It helped, of course, to have gorgeous legs.

"As near simultaneously as possible," he answered. "I don't mean we have to both talk at once, but that we both talk on whatever the reading is—literature or law. Is that all right with you?"

"Sounds lovely," Kate said.

"Do I catch an ironic note?" he asked. "I was told you wear irony the way some women wear perfume."

He had begun to flirt, a younger man with a woman just the right number of years older.

"It's a good defense," she said. "Against many things. Oddly enough, the only thing I find it difficult to be ironic about is the misuse of words for no decent reason."

"What words, though I hardly dare to ask? I probably misuse them all."

"Since you ask, *disinterested* to mean *uninterested; transpired* to mean *happened;* and a recent candidate, *serendipitously* to mean *by chance*. Now that I have established myself as a pedant, have you had any ideas about particular texts, or legal briefs, if that's what they're called?"

"Yes, I have," he said, obviously trying to remember if he had misused these words, and producing some papers just in time almost to collide with the waiter serving their first course. He handed her the sheets of paper. "These are the legal readings I thought we might use. *Michael M. v. Superior Court*, for instance, is a case of statutory rape which might go with some novel or other. About the rights of a woman to say no and mean it."

"Jude the Obscure," Kate said. "I think this is going to be possible. But isn't reading a case—how long is a case?—and a novel all at once rather a monumental assignment?"

"That's what we need to work out. I was hoping you would turn out to be an authority on shorter works of fiction. Or even chapters, if one can suggest so unliterary a practice."

"Give me a minute," Kate said. "I've no doubt we can work it out, but could we look for a moment at the larger picture? The law school, I mean, into which we are going to shoehorn this fascinating course."

"Of course. Shall I start at the beginning, anyway, the place where I come in?"

"The beginning is often a good place to start," Kate said solemnly. "I somehow get the impression that the Schuyler Law School is not exactly the cat's pajamas, but no one has told me why, apart from the fact that it isn't Harvard or Yale. Fact and frankness will be welcome."

"Fair enough. I'm really delighted that Reed is going to do a clinic for us. You're more luck than I had dared to hope for, or to imagine that the guardian angels of women's rights and minority culture might grant."

"Let's get to the angels later," Kate said. "Let's start with where you come in. Although," she felt constrained to add, not believing in angels, but not wanting to offend any should they somehow hover, "Reed's doing the clinic certainly does seem to have taken a certain amount of intervention on your part, and if the angels helped, so much the better. Proceed, please."

"Let's begin with the faculty," he said. "All male, and all certain that what they don't know and believe isn't worth knowing. I hardly have to describe them, except that they are beginning to smell the danger of new ideas and are rallying the troops. Or, as they say where I used to live, the wind is rising."

"Well, I gather it's not a law school anyone thinks of as prestigious," Kate said between mouthfuls. "Is this the same dynamic as in terrible schools in English novels; the worse the school, the crueler the teachers?"

"You may be right; I did spend two days with *Nicholas Nickleby* when it was on Broadway. But law schools are a little different. Unprestigious, Schuyler Law may be, but most of the faculty got their degrees at Harvard Law or Yale Law or Chicago Law and have been floating on that fact ever since. Maybe they published a casebook; they haven't published anything else. They don't really *think*, in my opinion, but they insist on all the old ways that have served so many years and ought to go on serving in a sane—that is, white—male world. Almost half the students are women, of course, and many of the students are minorities, but that's all the more reason to imbue them with the law as it should be practiced."

"Have there been many rumbles from the women and minorities?" Kate asked as her main course was served. "Are the masses stirring?"

"But little. These students are not your pampered darlings from Harvard and Yale, princes of all they survey. They've made it this far by the skin of their teeth, and they aren't inclined to interfere with their eventual law degree and job. One can hardly blame them. That's why I think the faculty needs to take a stand. Which was what Nellie Rosenbusch and I did."

"Nellie Rosenbusch?" Kate asked.

"The woman faculty member who was killed by a truck. Harriet and I are very suspicious."

"Oh, yes, of course," Kate said. "I don't think I ever heard her name."

"Nellie was a thorn in the faculty's side. She was even beginning to get some of the women students behind her. They—the outraged faculty—used everything they could against her, they didn't miss a trick, from sexual harassment to the silent treatment that I understand is what they do at West Point."

"But she did have tenure?"

"Yes, she did, I should have mentioned that. She got tenure the year I did, and she got it because of me. We let it be known that her qualifications were as good as mine, in fact better, and that I was willing to join her in a suit claiming so. They decided the easiest way out of that was to give it to us both. She was the first tenured woman in the place, if you can believe it. And they thought once she had joined the club, so to speak, she would shut up and go away. But she didn't."

"And you think they killed her; shoved her under a truck and brushed their hands, saying 'That takes care of *that*!'" Kate put down her fork. "Have you any evidence," she said, "apart from motive, opportunity, and your deep suspicions?"

"It's not circumstantial evidence, God knows. She landed in front of the truck, one of those high babies, and the driver never saw her. She wasn't a very big person." He paused for a moment.

"Is there any evidence that she was pushed?" Kate repeated.

"People waiting with her for the light think she must have been, because of the way she sort of collapsed all of a sudden. But no one saw exactly what happened. All eyes were on Nellie and the truck; all anyone remembers are the screeching brakes after she was hit. The police have done their best, but there's damn little evidence really, apart from the fact that there's no reason on earth why she should have fallen like that. They did the usual autopsy and there were no obvious health problems—heart attack, liquor, drugs, nothing like that."

"I hope Reed and I aren't expected to find out the truth about her death," Kate said. "I know I've investigated things from time to time, but I want to make sure that we're coming to teach a course and run a clinic. We're not expected to run an investigation, are we?"

"Certainly not. My only hope is that in this course we may be able to spread a little basic feminism around, and suggest that if law and literature can speak to each other, so can law and life. As it's lived, I mean, not as it turns up in the final published opinion. That's why I want to go back and look at the cases we teach from the beginning, look at the depositions and the stories, not just at the briefs and the opinions. Maybe we can do a case one week and a novel the next. Something like that."

"Well," Kate intoned, " 'I'm more than ever of the opinion that a decent human existence is possible today only on the fringes of society.' Hannah Arendt said that; wrote it, in fact, to Jaspers. I'm inclined to agree. And a revolution at Schuyler Law sounds as near to the fringes as I can get without leaving academia altogether."

"Perhaps," he said, "we ought to talk about schedules. What day of the week are we going to do this?"

"It's up to you," Kate said, "seeing as how you're taking it as part of your usual schedule. I can probably make it any day, as long as it's the afternoon, or at least very late in the morning."

"Good. How's Wednesday?"

"The very day I would have preferred," Kate said. "Wednesday is such a nice, middle day, so neatly balanced on both sides of the workweek."

"Wednesday afternoon it is. If it's all right with you, I'll arrange the hour and the room. Now, shall we have an exam or a paper?"

"Oh, let's have an exam," Kate said. "I never give exams, and I read too many papers in my line of work. Besides, if we word the questions carefully, we may actually find out what they've learned from us."

"I warn you, that may be a shock."

"I've said my prayers. It's too late now to worry about shocks. Are you planning to give me all those papers?"

"If you can bear it. They're the cases I thought we might use, around which I hope you will drape the proper literary texts. Literary critics are allowable, if they can be read without a French dictionary."

"Well," Kate said, taking the stack of paper from him, "I'll do my best. What are we calling the course?"

" 'Women in Law and Literature' is what I thought of. Simple, direct, and allowing almost any discussion of anything."

"And less likely to flutter the dovecotes than something with *feminism* in the title."

"I see you're getting the picture."

Kate leaned back in her chair and gazed at him, openly and frankly. He looked back with those bright, blue eyes. Don't worry, they promised, this isn't going to lead anywhere but to a small, local awakening in a brain-dead law school. Your husband's coming to dear old Schuyler Law, too; nothing to worry about for a minute.

This was all of course unsaid, but Kate heard it just the same. The trouble is, she told herself, I'm vulnerable now. Anything can push me off my center; anything can offer excitement of the sort that means one doesn't really have to ask oneself what the hell she thinks she's doing.

"Do you have an envelope for all these?" she said, lifting the papers.

"Sorry. Of course I do. Let me put you in a taxi." He waved for the check. God only knew, Kate thought, what he made at that law school and if he could really afford this dinner. But the Oak Room with all its elegance had been his idea; perhaps the law school was paying. She had, when you came right down to it, been recruited, and perhaps he wanted to make an agreeable impression. Anything a step above McDonald's would have done for her, or even someone's office, but he could not have known that.

"I think I'll walk," she said as they waited for his credit card to be returned, "even having to lug all this." She hefted the envelope he had given her. "Lawyers do churn out paper, don't they? But I like walking after dinner. It clears the sinuses."

"You think it's safe?"

"Nothing's safe. But Fifty-ninth Street and then Broadway is quite all right at this hour. I only walk on streets I know and trust, which is more than I can say about the people I teach courses with." Her smile softened the words.

Together they made their way out onto Fifty-ninth Street. Kate hoped he would not offer to walk with her, and he did not. That he knew the evening had accomplished all that could have been accomplished, and that further conversation would be tiresome, spoke well for him. Well, she could hear Reed saying, legal cases should be a pleasant change from *Middlemarch*.

Reed didn't say it when she got home, because she said it for him.

"Of course," she added, "one can always start with Susan Glaspell's 'A Jury of Her Peers,' one of those basic feminist texts, ignored for years, which tells the whole story."

"Even I know it," Reed said. "The men bumble around, and the women work out what really happened, because they know how to notice things and interpret the clues. It's about proud male assumptions versus modest female observation. Right?"

"Do I catch a disdainful note?" Kate said. "Now, don't you start giving me trouble. What about your clinic?" she asked, neatly passing the buck.

"It is going to be prisons. One of the benefits left over from my DA days is that I have a ready path to the head of the Board of Correction and, it is hoped, from there to state prisons. Anyway, with or without connections, it's going to be the state prison on Staten Island, half men and half women. Of the women, perhaps a tenth killed their husbands. You know, Kate, it wasn't until I realized, thanks to you, how at loose ends I was that the possibility of this clinic suddenly loomed as something I very much wanted to do."

"If you say so; what exactly will you do in your clinic at old Schuyler Law?"

"The students will study about the criminal justice system and represent prisoners. We'll take habeases and cases against the prison about conditions, like inadequate medical care and lack of safety. Eventually the students will appear in court, before administrative agencies like the parole board, for instance. Of course, we practice first, we have moots."

Kate's eyebrows shot up with humorous exaggeration.

"Really, Kate, if you're going to teach in a law school, you have to pick up a bit of the lingo. Moots are practice trials, and moot court, my love, is a sacred rite of a law-school education. I suspect even dear old Schuyler Law has them."

"How many students in a clinic?" Kate asked, ignoring the temptation to persiflage. Badinage was the spice of their marriage, and Kate enjoyed it, but sooner or later one had to get down to practical matters.

"I've said ten students at the most, but they'll probably give me twelve to be sure I have an overload. It's the sort of thing these guys would do."

"You mean these poor prisoners' only chance of getting legal help is ten or twelve first-year law students?"

"Second year," Reed said. "And without those students and the clinic, they wouldn't have any chance at all. Of course I go to court with them; usually the students are wonderful, but sometimes a professor, me, has to speak up in court and say 'Let me add something.' Not often, if all goes well."

"Explain to me again," Kate said, "who these prisoners are exactly. Besides battered wives and illegal immigrants. You see, I have been listening."

"Often prisoners have been told to plead guilty when they shouldn't have, or serious errors occurred at the trial. Most of them are guilty of something, but not necessarily fairly convicted or sentenced."

"Why?"

"Because the lawyers assigned to them have more cases and fewer resources than they should and can't manage; some of them don't know shit from shinola, or didn't care; didn't take the time to work out what ought to be done. Many assigned lawyers are great; some aren't. Not all ignorant lawyers are public defenders, either, though I may have left you with that prejudiced impression from my days at the DA's office. A lot of public defenders are damn good. In fact, they tend to get better lawyers than the DA's office, because public defending is not a step toward higher things. John F. Kennedy, Junior, chose to be a DA, not a public defender."

"I'm with you so far."

"That's about it. Doubtless you'll hear particulars as we begin our new legal life together. There are all sorts of problems like prisoners being denied visitors for some unlawful reason—a wife has a record, that sort of thing."

"I still don't see why you couldn't do this in a clinic on your home ground if it interests you so much."

"I helped out from time to time with different clinics— discrimination, Title VII, class suits, gay rights, the rights of assembly. I told you that the school didn't want to let me do a prison clinic, but the terrible truth, Kate, may be that I was too conventional to press hard. It took Blair's invitation to get me started. After all, I was an important person on the regular faculty. Such an important person that Schuyler is willing to invite me, even for a clinic they probably aren't gleefully anticipating. You see, I am changing, and how right you were about what had become of me."

"What day are you doing your clinic? Blair and I teach on Wednesday afternoons."

"Really, Kate, one doesn't do clinics on one day like seminars. When the trial's on, or when you have an appointment to meet with a prisoner or a judge, you go. *Every* day is nearer the mark."

"Well, you can report to me on prisons and I can report to you on feminist insurgency. At least we won't be graveled for lack of matter."

"Kate, you can't think we ever were lacking in conversation."

"It's supposed to be the inevitable destiny of married couples. We've noticed them in restaurants."

"We have never for one moment run out of conversation in a restaurant." He sounded quite put out.

"The question for now," Kate said, reaching out to touch him, "is what literature Blair and I are going to read with all these cases. Do you think law is ahead of literature in the matters of women's rights?"

"No, my dear Kate, it is not. But start with 'A Jury of Her Peers,' and then take up the case of the woman in Florida who beat her husband to death in her nightgown—that is, she was in her nightgown, not her husband—after he took up with another woman and insisted on leaving her, and she was convicted by a jury of all men."

"Are you making this up?"

"You overestimate me," Reed said. "*Hoyt v. Florida;* she sued on the basis of having had an all-male jury, but she lost. The right to women on a jury was won later by a man from Louisiana appealing because there were no women on the jury. Making men the argument for equal treatment between the sexes is a good ploy. Ask your Blair Whitson about it; he should know."

"He better," Kate said. "And he's not my Blair Whitson, he's yours."

She hoped Reed wasn't going to worry about Blair Whitson. Why should I think he would worry about Blair Whitson, Kate asked herself, when he never worried about anyone before? Because I am worried about Blair Whitson, Kate ruefully admitted. And I never found out if he was married. Please god he is. Or gay, of course, she added. That would do nicely.

Kate had gone back to reread le Carré after Harriet had mentioned him with such enthusiasm, starting at the beginning with Smiley's first adventures. She had paused, with sudden amusement, over a remark in one of Smiley's later cases: "Not of course that she knew anything, but what woman was ever stopped by a want of information." Touché, George, she thought, and especially now.

4

For the first time she was afraid of making a fool of herself, afraid of becoming involved in unlikely explanations with angular, suspicious people.

—JOHN LE CARRÉ
A MURDER OF QUALITY

"And this," Blair said, "is the seminar room we'll be using. I'm sorry it's in the basement, but there aren't many seminar rooms in this establishment. We'll be a nice change, us and a few eager students around a table, you at one end, me at the other. We've got about twenty students, by the way."

"And why are they taking our seminar?" Kate reasonably asked.

"Because they suspect it will be easier than some other electives, and they like me, not for my blue eyes but because I occasionally remember their names without looking at a chart. And I don't call on them unless they raise their hands. You," he added with a certain wry effort at gallantry, "are an object of curiosity, insofar as they allow themselves to indulge in that time-wasting emotion. And some of them will be the few really good students, returnees mostly, who come here bravely and go on to do fine things."

"Thanks," Kate said. "You've cheered me up considerably."

It was Kate's first day at Schuyler Law. The faculty was in the habit of holding a cocktail party, really a reception for the students, to mark the new semester; Blair had urged Kate and Reed to attend. "It's supposed to be for the students," he had explained, "and is compulsory for the faculty. In fact, the party's developed into a kind of reunion of buddies, the sort I've always imagined is enjoyed by an army unit or a fraternity group now well into middle age. Many of the students do come, feeling the time was well spent if their absence might be held against them, but most of the second- and third-year students skip it, pleading other compelling engagements."

Kate had arrived early to be shown the seminar room and Blair's office, which they were going to share. "Visiting faculty women, however exalted, do not rate offices around here," Blair said. "I hope you don't mind."

"It's you who should mind. Won't I be an intrusion?"

"Any intrusion is bearable one day a week. In the case of this particular intrusion, I expect eagerly to anticipate that day." They had made their way from the basement floor to the higher floor devoted to offices. Blair flung open a door, held it while waving her inside with a flourish, closed it, and sat down on a chair while pointing her to its mate opposite.

"My office," he said.

Kate sat down and looked around with frank curiosity. When she had canvassed the books and the view, she let her eyes stray to a picture of a woman on his desk.

"Your wife?" she asked. It seemed the most direct and the best way, although to what she was uncertain.

"Yes," Blair said. "But we're divorced. She decided she preferred a lawyer who made a bit more a year—well, a lot more a year. I keep her picture there to dissuade me from any impulsive moves toward marriage. We're quite friendly; she even admits that I'm more interesting than her present husband, and I refrain from pointing out the difficulty of finding anyone less interesting than her present husband. Enough of that. Shall we descend to the cocktail party? Perhaps if we were to arrive early, it would indicate a certain enthusiasm on your part that might well be worth the effort."

"Surely they can't object to me as much as all that?" Kate said.

46

"They object to you on the purest, frankest grounds of sexism. They're much more worried by Reed and his clinic. Not only has it shown up the lack of other nonsynthetic clinics, it always makes the Schuyler faculty nervous when the students are in danger of getting ideas."

"I hope we may prove a danger by inculcating ideas," Kate stiffly said.

"Let's hope."

"Blair," Kate said, "I'm not sure that you or anyone else can quite believe my ignorance about law schools. I don't even know what you ordinarily teach. I know Reed teaches criminal law, but I don't really know what that is, apart from reading the ever-drearier newspapers."

"Ah," Blair said. "What is criminal responsibility? That, as someone said, is the question. You don't know, I don't know, Reed probably has some idea, and I promise you no one at Schuyler Law has a clue, except to agree with Rehnquist and Scalia on all points, including instant implementation of the death penalty."

"That the faculty of Schuyler is hardly on the cutting edge of progressive thought I have more or less gathered. What I need," Kate said, "is a short rundown on the cast of characters before I meet them."

"Like the beginning of one of those old-fashioned, voice-over films, I suppose," Blair snorted.

"I like voice-over films," Kate said. "I know they're not in fashion, but they seem very British and interesting to me; so much better than the avant-garde sort where you can't figure out what happened or hear what anybody's saying until the end and often not even then."

"Good," Blair said, "because this is definitely an old-fashioned film. Let us start with contracts."

"Our contracts?" Kate said. "They're only for a semester, thank god."

"The course contracts," Blair said. "Has Reed told you nothing about law school?"

"Nothing," Kate said. "He would have, but I never asked. He doesn't teach it, so it never came up. Reed teaches criminal procedure; I have heard about that. Sometimes he teaches evidence."

"Doesn't he teach any first-year subject?" Blair asked.

"Only on occasion, I think. Except for those who request it, they alternate on first-year courses."

"O Reed, among the blessed. At Schuyler Law, everybody teaches the basic courses."

"And they are?" Kate firmly said. "I await your voice-over."

"The other basic courses," Blair said, "—I trust you are taking notes, I'm not going to repeat this, ever—are, in addition to Contracts: Constitutional Law, Criminal Law, Property, Procedure, and Torts."

"We're moving right along," Kate said cheerfully. "I've now got the six basic courses, and I have no intention of asking you about advanced courses. We'll save those for another time."

"To which I look passionately forward," Blair said. "All law-school courses are advanced, but some are core and some are not. That is, the core courses are taken by all students regardless of their interests in other areas of legal study, whereas the noncore advanced courses are taken according to the special interests of the students."

"So what do they do in clinics?" Kate asked. "And why has Schuyler had only synthetic ones?"

"Don't be a snob," Blair said. "Synthetic clinics teach much the same as real clinics. They're both involved with lawyerly skills. But Reed's kind of clinic—about which I'm frankly even more of a snob than you—teaches substantive law by working with students, clients, administrative agencies, or courts in a particular area of law. Simulated clinics only get you so far; they're okay for practice, but they don't provide help to real people in need."

"That's just what Reed said. On to the basic courses at Schuyler Law."

"Contracts." Blair took a break while (apparently) trying to picture the catalog description. "Contracts studies the laws regulating agreements for commercial purposes. It also studies how the state enforces contracts. That's a lot to study, and it always occupies two semesters. As does constitutional law."

"Don't tell me," Kate said, "let me guess. It studies the Constitution."

"Well done," Blair responded. He was getting into the spirit of the thing. "It also considers the legislative and judicial spheres, federal and state, government and individuals."

"In short," Kate said, "Rehnquist vs. Brennan, or Marshall vs. Thomas."

"You could put it that way, yes," Blair agreed. "Except that questions of original intent get rather hairy."

"Sorry for the uncalled-for remark," Kate said.

"Apology accepted. I'm doing my humble best."

"You're doing wonderfully," Kate told him, meaning it. "As to what you learn in Torts," she said, "I cannot even guess."

"Well, I have taught it," Blair said, "but that's not going to be much help. It's to do with injuries not covered by criminal law. It also deals with the principles of liability."

"What do you teach, besides literature and law with me?" Kate asked. "I should have asked that question long ago. Were you in literature, I would have ascertained your field in the Oak Room before we had ordered a drink. There is too little understanding between the professions."

"A condition we are trying to remedy with our lit-law course," Blair gallantly said. "I teach Procedure. Who can sue whom? When? What do courts do? What are the rules, the role of lawyers, the costs? Perhaps we can discuss the details some other time over a drink."

"That would be lovely," Kate said. "Now, what does that leave us? No, don't tell me; I've got to get this clear. Property; how could I forget?"

"In an American law school you can't and shouldn't. Some forward-looking schools actually include environmental as well as historical and economic perspectives. At Schuyler, they study property, meaning land and water, chiefly in the context of mine versus yours and, above all, versus the state. And speaking of Schuyler, we'd better get down to that reception. Follow me."

"Do they serve alcoholic beverages to oil the wheels of social intercourse?" Kate asked, remembering her recent visit to the Theban.

"That they do," Blair said. "Bourbon is the drink of choice."

"I should have guessed," Kate said. "It figures. Reed and I drink scotch."

"They'll probably run to a small allowance of scotch for you and Reed. I'm a scotch drinker myself." He bowed her out of the office, locking the door behind him.

The reception turned out to be much less difficult than any of them had anticipated, largely because of the alcohol. Kate, despite her questions to Blair concerning alcohol, decided not to drink, feeling the need to connect the names she hardly knew with the courses she had just heard about, and wanting to get an impression that might not be offered to her again. Kate never drank when she was working. She considered this reception, unlike that at the Theban, work. Why, I wonder? she asked herself.

Blair introduced Kate to Professor Zinglehoff, who immediately intrigued her. He had two characteristics she found compelling, in the sense in which a horror scene is compelling. First, Zinglehoff never finished a sentence, always interrupting himself just before the eagerly anticipated end to introduce another qualification, and second, he wore under his dark jacket a black turtleneck sweater instead of a shirt and tie, which made him look exactly like a turtle. A tendency to thrust his head forward as he made his never syntactically concluded points increased the resemblance. Kate, who liked turtles, tried to turn this aspect into a compliment, but faltered. My god, she thought, I'm describing someone without even meaning to. But Zinglehoff is someone deserving of description; just think what Dickens might have made of him.

"It must be a new experience, being taught by a woman," Zinglehoff remarked, "not that there is anything untoward about a woman teaching in a law school, particularly a woman who is not a lawyer, and many intelligent women are not lawyers, in fact, I suppose you could say most intelligent women are not lawyers, but I have been curious as to how our students, who are a hardworking lot, particularly when you consider their outside jobs, and some of them are women like yourself—"

"What do you teach?" Kate rudely interrupted. She wondered how his wife, if any, managed to converse with him. Perhaps she left notes. Perhaps at home he was unalterably silent. One could only guess. "Do you teach a basic course?"

"Basic courses are, of course, the heart of any law school, unlike all those frills that can be added afterward, well, some of them are useful, I don't doubt it, in their own way, and I have even taught Real-Estate Transactions from time to time, when the need arose, which in a small school like ours it sometimes does, due to leaves and other emergencies, and I can't say that I approve of hiring adjunct professors to take up the—"

"You teach Property?" Kate asked. She felt an overwhelming urge to shout, "Answer yes or no." And indeed, a yes, trailing a long sentence behind it, had just passed his lips when Reed appeared to the rescue, saying: "Kate, Professor Abbott would like to meet you. He's over there; let me introduce you."

"Excuse me," she said to Zinglehoff.

"You looked in need of rescue," Reed said, "and Abbott did ask to meet you. Be brave." He grinned, and headed her toward Professor Abbott, who was indeed notable; in addition to being the only nonwhite person in the room, he was large, and handsome, and stately.

"You're not a lawyer," he informed Kate, shaking her hand. "Blair Whitson has tried to explain to me why we want a nonlawyer teaching in a law school, but I'm afraid I didn't altogether get the picture. Could you clarify it for me? I'd be grateful."

"Certainly," Kate said. She looked at her empty glass.

"Let me get you another drink," Abbott said. "What was it? Gin?"

"I've had enough," Kate said, "but thank you for the offer. Actually, I was looking into my glass for inspiration to answer your question rather than for a drink."

"I know," Abbott surprisingly said, "you think I'm an 'old boy,' as my daughter calls all academics my age, and I proudly proclaim that indeed I am. It is a privilege for me to be here, in such a fine law school, and I would like to see it continue to offer what I was so glad to be allowed to learn when I went to law school many years ago."

"And instead they are offering the sort of irrelevance I teach," Kate said. "I see your point, I really do."

"It isn't alone what you teach," Abbott said. "It's what the students seem to expect these days. They don't come to learn, they come to argue before they know what they're arguing about. They know how to challenge but not how to acquire the information that gives them the right to challenge. Very old-fashioned, isn't it?"

"No," Kate said, rather liking him. "It's gone too far, I do see that. Even in literary studies, many students don't want to study texts or, as we used to say, literature, they want to discuss the social, cultural, gender, and economic conditions surrounding and infusing the text. One can't help feeling annoyed with this shift in emphasis from time to time, but I tend to look on it as an extreme but necessary intergenerational adjustment."

"That's put magnanimously," Abbott said. "But why did this extreme adjustment just happen lately? Generations of students studied law as it was taught, and they probably studied literature that way, too. Why need we change so dramatically? Are you sure you wouldn't like another drink?"

"Well, I might get some more tonic," Kate said, moving toward the bar.

"Allow me," Abbott said; he took her glass. "I'll be right back; don't move. Just plain tonic?"

"Please," Kate said. His gallantry allowed her a moment to structure her response, for which she was grateful.

"I've been thinking of what you asked," she said when he had returned with their glasses refilled. "I don't think revolutions come gradually, or in measured steps, and we are living in a revolution. There are two possible faculty responses to revolutions: to fight them, and to join them, hoping in the process perhaps to offer not only encouragement, but some restraint and caution. The problem I have found—I speak frankly, and only about literature—is that caution is misplaced, because those in power, those who like the old ways, will not budge until pushed. And once you push, the momentum carries you even further than you had quite foreseen."

"Yes," Abbott said, "I've noticed that. That's why I'm against the pushers. I'm ready to stand and defend what we have. After all, it took many years of effort to achieve what we have, in law and literature, and surely it's worth respect."

"Except for the fact that it is white men who have achieved it, and told some lies and committed some crimes in the process. Since we now know that, we revolutionaries feel inclined to question everything, perhaps more than we should."

"You want to throw out the baby with the bathwater?"

"No," Kate said. "I think we just want to reconsider the baby and change the bathwater. But clichés are hard to build on, don't you find?"

"Clichés, perhaps. Wisdom, I find, is not hard to build on." He had returned to his pomposity, and was looking over her shoulder. Kate turned to find Blair approaching with yet another faculty member in tow. "Let me introduce you to Augustus Slade," he said to Kate. "Kate Fansler is teaching the law and literature course with me," Blair told Slade, unnecessarily. More informatively, and sensing her need to distinguish these men one from the other, he said to Kate: "Professor Slade teaches Criminal Law." Kate greeted Slade with more enthusiasm than she felt; one could have too many conversations with members of this exalted faculty. She wondered, irrelevantly, if Harriet had decided to attend this sad example of a social whirl. Apparently not; wise Harriet.

Kate repressed a sigh. When caught, as she now was, in a reception or cocktail party, Kate thought of Shaw's response when asked to stand for Parliament: "It would be easier and pleasanter to drown myself," he had replied. But Professor Slade was, clearly, ready like the others to let her know she had no business here at a law school. What Slade did not realize was that Kate had decided upon him as the one to be questioned about the battered woman syndrome. Reed had told her that a number of women in the prison his clinic would be associated with were there for having killed their battering husbands. Kate wondered how the old guard would react to this new twist of the law, though she thought she could guess.

"And how do you like the company of lawyers?" Slade asked. "Or are you, because of your lawyer husband, quite used to having us around?"

"I'm not used to it," Kate said, "and I welcome the opportunity to talk about law instead of literature. Would you mind if I asked you some lawyerly questions? Blair did say you teach Criminal Law."

"Like your husband. Surely you can't have any questions you couldn't ask him?"

That was a facer. "Well," Kate said, adopting a simpering manner that always worked with just-met professors and other self-satisfied and powerful males, "I don't like to bother him with questions when he comes home after a hard day's work. One wants to show an interest, don't you know, but one doesn't want to hammer away."

"Very good thinking," Slade said. "I wish you could pass your wisdom on to my wife. She seems to think I can explain every legal twist and turn the newspapers pepper us with. What was it you wanted to ask in these professional surroundings?"

"Well," Kate simpered on, "being a woman, I'm naturally interested in the new laws affecting women. The old laws don't seem to have taken women into account." She hoped this would get him onto the battered woman syndrome, but if not, she would have to get more specific.

It appeared, however, that she had pushed the right button. "These changes in the law are preposterous nine tenths of the time," he declared. "Giving women total rights over their bodies is bad enough, with no consideration for the fetus, but when you distort the law to let a woman murder her husband and let her off by rules that don't apply to men, you have got yourself in real danger. Real danger."

"Surely that can't happen," Kate said, widening her eyes and crossing several fingers and toes.

"It can and does, my dear. Practically every day. It might have happened to my oldest friend, Fred Osborne, but the only comforting aspect to his horrible death is the fact that his wife was sent to the prison on Staten Island before this battered-woman nonsense took hold, and I trust she will rot there. Betty Osborne should have been put to death, in my opinion, but despite what you say, the law is easier on women."

Kate forswore pointing out that New York State did not have the death penalty except for killing policemen. "I can't believe that the wife of a friend of yours actually killed her husband," she said.

"Killed him in cold blood when he was asleep. Just as though he were an animal. Like a gang execution, really, that's what it was. Horrible."

"Why was she mad at him?" Kate asked.

"No reason; no reason on earth. She was just crazy, a mad, un-grateful, unbalanced woman."

"Did he beat her? Isn't that why it's called the battered woman syndrome?"

"Of course he didn't beat her; he was a member of this faculty, not a working-class thug. She claimed he beat her, of course, but I can tell you the worst he did was drink a bit much, and maybe he knocked her around once or twice when he was under the influence, but I'm sure she wasn't battered. She had a nice home and two children; she was a liar and a nut, if you ask me. Now, if you'll excuse me." Slade left with no pretense of courtesy; he was opting out of the discussion.

Kate stood for a moment, reflecting on his remarks, isolated in this room of babbling voices, sharply aware of not belonging, of being, in fact, a spy in an enemy camp. She had barely begun to reflect on this strange experience when a glass was tapped, and a tall, trim, handsome man demanded attention. "Welcome," he said, when the room grew quiet, "welcome to our traditional gathering. At least once each semester we join, all of us who teach in this fine institution, in one room to remind ourselves who we are and what our mission is: to pass on the law as our forefathers conceived it, to the young who will defend it after we are gone. The need for defense of that noble law grows greater each year. I lift my glass in tribute to those who honor what time and experience have proven true to our country's destiny."

Kate found Blair at her side. "Who on earth . . . ?" she whispered.

"The dean, our leader," Blair whispered back. "You should have met him when you were hired, but he was busy fund-raising. Frankly, I rather pushed you through before his return. He doesn't believe in law and literature, or in law and anything else whatsoever, including justice." The dean droned on praising his law school for "maintaining standards too easily abandoned by institutions considered more elite, who had sold out to the demands of those marginal to our great culture, who had no hand in writing our laws or defending them against their enemies. I drink to the wise makers of our Constitution."

"Does he consider the Bill of Rights part of the Constitution?" Kate asked.

"I doubt it," Blair said. "He would certainly not be in favor of them, were they up for a vote today. He thinks the Second Amendment guarantees his and every American's right to carry an unlicensed handgun."

"My god, Blair, what have we got into, me and Reed? How did you ever decide to join this mob in the first place?"

56

"I wanted to be in New York, a city I love. Of course, as you realize, I had no idea what I was getting into. So, instead of leaving, I decided to bore from within. Hence you and Reed."

The dean was concluding his remarks to enthusiastic applause. All raised their glasses to drink to their fine school. Kate thought there was a distinct danger that she might be ill; she and Blair made their way out of the room and, eventually, out of the building. Kate took large breaths of air.

"And to think I might have drunk with them," she said. "I'm particular about whom I drink with, and it doesn't include this amazing faculty. Slade actually told me that one of his noble colleagues was shot by his wife when he was sleeping. Is that true? Slade said she shot her husband like a gang executioner."

"Gangs execute in the back of the head; she shot him in the chest," Blair said. "A few times. And yes, of course I know about it and it is true. He does seem to have been a monster, but as far as the faculty here is concerned, he was the innocent victim of a woman's wrath."

"I begin to think I know nothing about crime," Kate said. "And she didn't try to hide the gun or pretend there had been a burglary, nothing like that?"

"Nothing like that. She called for help. They found her still holding the gun. She never denied killing him; he died before the medics could get there."

"Did you know her at all?" Kate asked.

"No. I'm afraid I rather avoided my colleagues after hours; certainly I didn't know their wives. Nellie Rosenbusch knew her, though. Said she often had bruises, and cried all the time. Nellie told me she never guessed Betty would have the nerve; she certainly didn't have the nerve to leave. There were children, of course."

Kate sighed. Reed, coming up to them at that moment, suggested to Kate that they proceed uptown. Like her, he seemed eager to place some distance between the party scene and himself. "Will you come with us?" he asked Blair.

But Blair felt he should return to the party. "I am on the faculty," he said. "I can't flit in and out like you two. See you in class anyway," he told Kate. She and Reed set out toward the subway.

"Shall we walk to the next stop?" he asked.

"I'm always ready to walk," Kate said. "Tell me more about your prospective battered-women clients who killed their husbands. No," she said, stopping in her tracks. "I think I'll go back and have a word with Harriet, who is supposedly to be found in the secretarial room, or whatever they call it. I want to get my impressions clear about the members of this creepy faculty before I forget which is which. Do you mind going on alone?"

"I will always mind going on alone," Reed said, "but I can handle it for a few hours."

After some exploration and the opening of a number of wrong doors, Kate found Harriet seated in a large room at the first desk she encountered upon entering. Behind her were other desks occupied by young women, sitting before computers; what Kate took to be copying machines were grouped together at the very back, as though for protection.

"You look surprised," Harriet said by way of a greeting.

"I am. Mere professors of literature do not get this kind of service. There are two sad and overworked women for the whole department. I type my own letters, simultaneously acquiring nobility for myself and accuracy for my letters."

"Lawyers are rich and catered to," Harriet said. "Blair Whitson told me that one of the things that used to infuriate Nellie Rosenbusch was that if she came in here to get something copied, any male professor in the room would assume she was a secretary and ask her to 'take care of this' for him."

"I can't help feeling, fresh as I am from the reception downstairs, that there ought to be one redeeming character in this place."

"One honest man, as the angel said before destroying Sodom. Or was it Gomorrah? We have Blair; that's miracle enough."

They were interrupted by a man, apparently liberated from the reception, asking for a clean copy of this and eighteen copies of that. Kate stood by while Harriet dealt with him.

"You seem good at this," Kate said.

"Of course I'm good at it; anyone with a modicum of intelligence and the patience of Griselda would be. We take all the hassle out of these men's lives; it's brought me to a new principle of leadership. No rich men should be leaders because they do not experience hassle, which is the major lot of most lives. Is there anything I can do for *you*, by the way, besides chatter on? Do you want something typed for your seminar?"

"What I want is some inside dope, bluntly put," Kate said. "Can you take a tea break or something?"

"Actually, we're just about done here." And Kate looked up to see the women turning off their computers and retrieving their purses from desk drawers. "Make it a scotch break, and I'm with you."

"Sold," Kate said. "Your place or mine?"

"Yours. You have better scotch. Also, as someone said of George Smiley, 'There has always been that certain kind of guilt about passing on his whereabouts—I still don't know why.' "

They arrived at Kate's house, where she was amused to see Harriet greet the doorman as an old acquaintance. Reed had left a note saying he had gone over to his office to get his mail.

"The truth is," Kate said when they were seated, scotch in hand and the bottle on the table, "I wanted to find out if you'd picked up a good bit of gossip while reigning over the secretarial room."

"But of course. To quote yet another of le Carré's characters, not dear George Smiley: 'Men are no good at it. Only women are capable of such passionate espousal of the destiny of others.' "

"It doesn't sound altogether a compliment," Kate said.

"It's still true. And what man is there who wouldn't talk to you with a little encouragement, or even with none? That being established, what sort of gossip were you after?"

"Professor Slade told me at the reception that one of the law professors there had been shot by his wife; she's in prison on Staten Island, where Reed's clinic will have its clients. I thought if you knew anything about it, he might be persuaded to look into the matter further. If she really was a battered wife, that is."

"She was battered all right," Harriet said. "Any number of the secretaries saw the evidence; so did Nellie. They all say he was such a bastard you could hardly believe."

"But beloved by his colleagues at Schuyler no doubt."

"No doubt. I'm told they testified on his behalf at her trial. They're a tight little bunch there. Isn't it wonderful how mediocrities support one another? I can never understand whether they're afraid of nonmediocrities or can't tell the difference."

"Most people can't tell the difference," Kate said.

"I can," Harriet snorted, "because, after all, I'm a gutsy aging woman. And as Donald Hall put it in his recent book of poems, 'Timidity encourages death and never prevents dying.' My motto; well put."

"It may be a fine motto for an older person," Kate said. "I don't think it's very good advice for an adolescent boy living in an inner city."

"I hate people who are always ready with a comeback," Harriet said, reaching for the bottle. "The only problem with you, Kate, is that you've never come up against a group of bonded males swollen with mediocrity enjoying power and set upon defending their turf. Maybe you've read about them in the newspapers; they're in the navy, they're in the Senate, they're in IBM and every other business. Did you happen to read about the dead feminist lawyer whom the *Law Review* boys at Harvard thought it so amusing to parody, with great cruelty, after her murder; they parodied Nellie at Schuyler in much the same way, doing their damnedest against individual women, dead or alive, and against feminism. I'm accused of exaggerating; but these men are so defensive they can't see where they're wrong, or even admit they might be mistaken. I don't know how much damage they did in my long-abandoned English department, but I think I can guess how much damage they can do in a law school."

"Life must be brutal in that secretarial room, to make you so angry. I'm afraid I just find them pitiful rather than dangerous. And not all conservative men are mediocre," Kate added, although she would have been hard put to understand why she was arguing with Harriet, whose rightness was eerily recognizable.

"Well, I do get carried away," Harriet said, smiling. "Protectors of the honored past may not be mediocre, but they are threatened, and threatened men are dangerous. They have had power for so long, they have been on the top of the hierarchy for so long, they can't believe that any justice can be involved in their loss of that cozy, high place."

"How and where," Kate asked, "do you read Donald Hall's latest book of poems?" She really wanted to know.

"In the public library. You can sit there and read and no one bothers you. It takes a while to get the books, of course, but I make lists and wait. I can't take them out; you need a card for that, and I'm determined to have used my phony name and documents only once. Anyway, I like reading in libraries, even the impoverished libraries New Yorkers are stuck with. I also read A. N. Wilson's biography of C. S. Lewis, about how his colleagues at Oxford hated him because he was both brilliant and wrote popular books, so that even he, a man, frightened them in their comfortable niches. I made a note of it."

Kate smiled as Harriet rummaged in her bag for her notebook. She found herself overcome with affection for Harriet, not least, she thought, because it was such fun arguing with the woman. Harriet retrieved her notebook with a satisfied yell, and flipped its pages. "Here we are," she said. "Wilson remarks that Lewis's works 'were far more interesting and distinguished than anything which his rivals for the job had produced. They, however, were safe men, worthy dullards, and this is usually the sort of man that dons will promote.' Dons and American professors, law or literature, it doesn't matter."

"Does that make Blair a dullard?" Kate asked.

"Good question," Harriet said. "I don't know. Sometimes when they hire young men, they make mistakes, and think because he has the right color, religion, sexual orientation, and education, he'll fit in. Ninety times out of a hundred, maybe more than that, he does. It pays, you see. Blair may just possibly be in the ten percent. After all, he was a friend of Nellie's, and he did get Reed to run a clinic; he is teaching with you, a renowned woman of perversity, and a course called Law and Literature at that. But he could, at any time, decide not to risk too much. Remember A. N. Wilson's words: 'Where mediocrity is the norm, it is not long before mediocrity becomes the ideal.' "

And so the semester got under way. Reed, it seemed to Kate, worked considerably harder at his clinic than she did on her course. Preparation for only one course a week was child's play, compared with her usual schedule, but the truth was that the class itself presented far more difficulty than Kate was used to. Blair explained it concisely: "We've given them permission to speak of their experiences, in and out of law school, which no other class has done. So, naturally, they take out their angers on us. Rather like parents with adolescent children, or so I would imagine. And rather like parents, we would dearly like to kick them from time to time."

Kate's reaction to the class, however, was less that of agonized parent than despairing academic. At least, she wryly thought, the old boys who run Schuyler Law classes by the Socratic method don't find their students arguing with every second sentence uttered.

It was not long after that something ominous happened.

Blair and Kate had finished teaching their class. Many of the students stayed on to talk to one another, or to the professors, but there were always a few who hurried to the door at the earliest possible moment. Today, however, the door was locked, and could not be opened. Nor did banging upon it produce any response whatever.

The room in the basement of the building had only one door and recessed windows, below grade and behind bars. The men who had tried to leave banged on the door, and soon began to kick it. Blair and Kate tried the handle themselves, recognized the uselessness of trying to force it open, and suggested, not without a certain pleasure, that everyone go on screaming as loudly as possible. Kate turned to Blair.

"Aren't there cleaners who come in the evening?"

"I think so; I've never really clocked them. And who knows if they penetrate to the basement." Looking around, he could see that the students were beginning to look alternately angry and afraid, a dangerous combination.

"Aren't the cleaning materials kept in the basement?" Kate asked.

"No," one of the students answered. "They're kept outside the entrance to the library. I've noticed them there when I was going out of the library for a smoke. For all we know, they may only clean the basement once a week, if then."

"Or once a month," another student said.

Kate, who was aware of a certain rising panic in herself, easily enough disguised and repressed, worried about the same response in the others, perhaps stronger and less easily restrained. She caught Blair's eye and could see that he was equally, and similarly, worried.

And then, as suddenly as it had started, the situation righted itself. One of the women students removed a cellular phone from the huge bag she carried about with her. "Who shall I phone?" she asked.

"Nine-one-one," came a chorus of voices.

After that they waited for the police, watching through the dirty windows and the bars. The police arrived and tried with a crowbar to force open the door; that failing, they removed the hinges. It occurred to Kate that they might have called a locksmith, which would have been more seemly. But no doubt the police were better for preventing panic. They had a bullhorn.

"All of you get to the back of the room, as far away from the door as you can get. Who's in charge of this class?"

"I am," Blair said, after exchanging a glance with Kate. After all, Kate thought, he does belong here; he is, rightfully, in charge. She appreciated Blair's consideration of his answer rather than his natural assumption of leadership. She looked at him so steadily, she momentarily forgot about the locked door.

"Okay," the bullhorn continued. "You, the one in charge, get everybody, I mean everybody, up against the wall farthest from the door. You got that?" Blair yelled back that yes, they got it, but it was doubtful if they could hear him.

They couldn't all fit against the wall, so they made two rows, the outer one pressing back against the inner one in a way that clearly added a certain spice to the whole adventure, which had, by now, with the arrival of the police, taken on the appeal of a lark.

"Ready?" the bullhorn thundered.

"Ready," Blair shouted, whether audibly to the police or not they could not tell. It certainly sounded loud enough to Kate to be heard in Staten Island. There was a moment of absolute silence, no one seemed to breathe, and then, in a wholly anticlimactic way, the door fell away. The police triumphantly entered, and the adventure was over.

But not entirely over, it soon appeared. The students left hastily, and with good humor—"always has been a class full of surprises," one of them said—and then the police entered the room. Again they asked who was in charge.

"We are," Blair said this time, pointing to himself and Kate. "We are."

When the police finally left, having taken their names with much other tedious information, Blair and Kate found themselves in a hilarious mood. "Come on up to my office," Blair said. "I haven't yet told you, but I keep a bottle there for moments exactly like this. Although," he added as they moved toward the stairs, "most of the moments requiring strong liquors are usually not as amusing as this, or as easily resolved."

"I wonder if it's really resolved," Kate said, when they had each got a drink and laughingly clinked their glasses. "Somebody locked that door. Perhaps we had better be careful they don't lock this one," she added, getting up to open it.

"Don't," Blair said, catching her hand and stopping her. "Don't open it just yet. Let's enjoy our lucky escape." He pulled her to him, gently, it might almost have been by accident.

"I'm going," Kate said, and went. Then of course she had to come back to collect her coat and her briefcase.

Blair smiled amiably. "Okay," he said. "Not to worry."

But Kate was worried. And not about locked doors. Well, she assured herself, about that, too. Naturally.

5

*Spying is eternal. . . . For as long
as rogues become leaders, we shall spy.*

—JOHN LE CARRÉ
THE SECRET PILGRIM

Reed, meanwhile, having written up the directions for the students taking the clinic, had found himself an assistant. She was a third-year student at Reed's law school, on her way to an associate's job at a Wall Street law firm and happy to spend the intervening time, while her law studies dwindled to a close, assisting Reed with his clinic. She had told him that she was assuaging her conscience by working with women in prison, and Reed told Kate that whatever her motives, she was a godsend: smart, organized, able to keep the students to their schedules without insulting anyone.

Reed asked her to have dinner with them—in a restaurant, of course, they entertained nowhere else—and Kate found the young woman delightful: down-to-earth, vigorous, obviously one of those exhausting individuals who jogged and pulled on machinery to strengthen their upper bodies, but frank and spritely, with a boyish charm and a girlish giggle. Her name was Barbara, but "everybody calls me Bobby."

"You don't look like the sort who would want to work in a corporate law firm," Kate said. "Not that I have the slightest idea really what type that is. More conventional, I thought, more given to suits with long jackets and short skirts, with their hair cut to look windblown." Bobby's hair was longish, gathered up on either side with combs, which, occasionally relinquishing their hold, allowed her hair to fall forward over her face.

"Oh, I shall have to conform," she said. "I might have been hired for my brains, but they'll only keep me for my conventional attitudes. As to why a corporate law firm, there are three reasons—money, money, and money. Loans to pay off, that sort of thing. Besides, since I hope to work for the president one day—Democratic, of course—I thought I should know how business firms operate."

"I oughtn't to have asked," Kate said. "You are kind to have answered so frankly."

"A pleasure," Bobby said, and seemed to mean it.

Kate told Bobby the story of their locked-in seminar, which, given its easy solution, induced a certain amount of hilarity. Then Reed and Bobby went on to discuss the running of their clinic, already well under way. Kate turned her attention to her food and was happy to listen to them in silence.

Yet pondering, later that night, on Blair, their class, and his reasons for initiating it, she decided that in the morning she would call him and ask to see him. There was too much about him that was still a mystery, and a few direct questions were certainly in order. By morning she still thought questioning him a good idea; she called, and was invited to join him in his office that afternoon. "I'd offer to meet you more uptown," he said, "but there's a faculty meeting I must be here for, more's the pity."

So Kate arrived at his office at the appointed hour.

"I know I've already asked, and you've already answered, my question about how you came to be here in the first place. At this inferior law school, I mean. Reed says you could certainly have found a job in a better place. Not that we've been discussing you," she hastily added, "but the question did come up."

"Why I came here in the first place," Blair said, bending a large paper clip out of shape as, years ago, he would have made quite a business of lighting a cigarette, "is an easy question. In fact, I've already told you the answer. I wanted to be in New York. The jobs I was offered elsewhere were not that exciting or that much better paid, though they were probably in better law schools. I was already itching to get out of my marriage, and my wife had an excellent job offer in St. Louis. She was as glad to get rid of me as I of her, in case you're wondering, but as a woman, she was less inclined to walk out of a relationship rather than endure it. New York and Schuyler Law seemed the way out of a lot of problems. I did get another offer soon after I arrived here, so this faculty offered me tenure, and I stayed. They thought I was one of them, and I was."

"Which brings me to a harder question. What brought about the change?"

Blair reached across the desk toward Kate on the other side and took her hand for a moment. Then he let it go, smiling at her as though making up his mind. "The beginning of the answer is easy enough," he said. "Bit by bit these guys began to turn my stomach. You know, like discovering caffeine gives you a headache; it takes quite a while before you are ready to admit that it's caffeine, and not a lot of other less important things. Their attitude toward the students, which was bad enough in class, was more disturbing at committee meetings. Men have always made remarks about women's bodies, and I just took them as par for the course, like remarks about 'niggers' and 'Jewboys' and 'Chinamen' in the old days. Once you're made aware of what you're saying, you can't believe you said it, but in fact you did: everyone did. So it wasn't that so much, it was their scorn of the students, as though they despised them or were putting something over on them. I'm not putting this too well."

"Well enough," Kate said.

"You have to understand it was all a rather slow process, to say the least. When you're a WASP male, there isn't much that you can't swallow; it's horribly easy not to think about it at all. And then Nellie came here to teach. I think they were getting antsy about questions being asked because they didn't have a woman on the faculty, so they hired her in case anyone brought the matter up. God knows the women students didn't bring it up. And the faculty already had its black. He was willing to be one of them—well, you've met him—so they thought they'd get a woman in just the same way."

"Did she take it all for granted, too, at first?" Kate asked.

"Not nearly as long as I did. For one thing, she was overwhelmed by the women students, who, however unraised their conscious-nesses, wanted a woman to talk to. It was a strain. They would get angry if she didn't make time for them, assuming her attention as their right, even though they wouldn't dream of making the same assumptions about a male teacher."

"I know enough about that to take it as read," Kate said. "Then what happened?"

"She made friends with me because I was the youngest male around, and not quite as set in my ways as the other guys. Oh, it began in the usual way. She asked if she could talk to me, and the next thing we knew we were in bed. It's funny, but these days we seem to go to bed first and talk afterward, almost as though we were getting it out of the way. Now AIDS is changing that. Anyway, we soon traded in the sex for companionship. At first I found her complaining a bit much, though she did try to contain it, but little by little it sank in—how she felt about teaching here, how the faculty treated her, and the problems with the students. Some of them became her friends, and a few actually began to support her and listen to *her* problems; not many, but a few. I guess it was all affecting me more than I realized. And then"—Blair seemed to be trying to return the clip to its original form—"we had moot court. I've never told this to anyone," he added. "I feel like an idiot."

"You were involved in the moot court?" Kate asked, to help him along.

"I was one of the faculty observing. There was a student there, a woman, who was a lot brighter, or maybe I ought to say less rough-edged, than most of our students, and she did a really brilliant job. Afterward I took her and another guy who'd won out for a drink.

Her happiness at having done so well, even in a half-assed place like this, was touching. Then she left us, and the guy and I walked off in the same direction. 'She really was into it, really excited about moot court,' he said. I thought he was appreciating her, but there was something about the chuckle I didn't like. I asked him how he knew. 'I could see her nipples were erect,' he said; 'she was hot.' And that, my dear Kate, is what did it. And I've never told that to a living soul."

Kate smiled at him. "Yes," she said, "you crossed the line."

"What line?"

"The line that makes men, a few men, understand what the whole women's thing is about. They cross over into another country, and they can never go back, or most of them can't. Because once you understand, you are doomed to understanding, and all the shit you take from other men doesn't change that. It's always interested me, and I always wondered if there was one moment that did it, like your moment."

"Did Reed have a moment?"

"You know, I've never asked him. Maybe I will someday."

"And," Blair said, "you had to ask me because you weren't sure I'd really crossed the line, wasn't sure that, as Harriet's le Carré world would say, I wasn't a mole."

Kate looked down at her hands in her lap.

"All right," Blair said, "don't spell it out. I don't blame you. There are times when even I wonder what I really believe. And despite your fine talk about crossing the line, if Nellie hadn't died under that truck, I might have crossed back. Well, I might," he insisted as Kate shook her head. "But I never believed in that accident. I'd walked with her enough, she was a real New Yorker, she knew New York drivers, she would never have stepped out into traffic that way. But who can really tell? She may have been upset, preoccupied. Anyway, I couldn't shut my eyes to the fact that she was causing a lot of questions to be asked around here. A few of the students, many of the women and some of the men, were not being as docile as they used to be. And let's face it, since her death those few students have reverted to their previous form."

"And," Kate said, rising, "I must allow you to revert to your previous form as a proper attender of faculty meetings." For a moment Blair seemed about to say something, but Kate left before he could decide exactly what to say. I'm getting into my detective mode, Kate said to herself; that's easy to see, but what am I detecting? She decided, since she was here, to call on Harriet.

The secretarial room was in full operation, with male faculty standing around making demands, and women scurrying here and there. Only Harriet, seated at her desk, retained a firm, unshakable demeanor. She greeted Kate formally, assuming, for any faculty observing them, that Kate had come with some manuscript to be dealt with. "Take a seat, Professor Fansler," Harriet said without so much as a blink.

"No rush," Kate answered, doing as she was bid.

Eventually the men cleared out, the women went to work, and Harriet approached Kate.

"Is there a women's room near here?" Kate asked.

"Certainly," Harriet said, rising. "I'll show you." And together they left the room, to regroup amid the sinks and stalls.

"What, ho?" Harriet asked when they were there.

"I wanted to ask some questions about Nellie," Kate said. "I know you weren't here when she was, but I can't very well ask anyone who was."

"Not even Blair?"

"Not more than I have already. I believe him," Kate said, "I really do. But I want a more unbiased report. What have you gathered?"

"Not a damn thing." Harriet washed and dried her hands. "Did you know that handling paper dries your hands? It was news to me, but I've come to believe it. The only thing I wondered about was if the police had checked alibis. You know, where were all the members of the faculty when she went under the truck? You'll never guess the answer."

"Let me try. Not one of them was anywhere that could be firmly established."

"Correct. Except for Professor Abbott, who was at the dentist, testified to by the dentist, the hygienist, and the receptionist. They might all have been in cahoots with him, but there were also other patients there who remembered him. Being black in most white surroundings makes him easily memorable, which must be beastly, but in this case was a benefit."

"The police told you all this?"

"Well," Harriet said, "I did rather misrepresent myself as a lawyer from another faculty. You needn't look so dubious; I have been on a faculty and can behave as pompously as any male, if circumstances so require. I said there was worry in the legal academic community, did these lawyers have alibis, and so on and so forth. They didn't tell me much, but they did tell me about the alibis, or the lack thereof. They also pointed out that this meant little; few people have alibis, and I understand that the possession of one always merits a closer look."

"Which Professor Abbott endured and passed?" Kate said.

"That's it. I had better get back to my duties. The women, who are bored to death with their work, poor dears, tend to chatter when left unattended, and the faculty men who drift in tend to become first bantering and flirtatious, and then peeved."

"Did Nellie have an office?" Kate asked.

"She did. I know that because I was asked, as an extension of my duties, to arrange for her personal belongings to be cleaned out of it."

"And what happened to what they cleaned out?"

"It's in the basement, in a box, waiting to be called for. So far, no one has. Her family scarcely wanted her leavings from this beastly place. Are you contemplating a snoop among them?"

"Yes."

"Good girl. I'm glad to see you're beginning to take an interest."

"I hope I'll be able to justify this sort of snooping; but she is dead, and one would rather like to know why. Not that I don't feel a certain moral pang, but in this place, I can subdue it rather easily. After all, it's no one's business but Nellie's, and I can't believe she would mind."

"In the very first book he wrote about Smiley, le Carré says: 'It was a peculiarity of Smiley's character that through the whole of his clandestine work he had never managed to reconcile the means to the end.' I think if you have the same peculiarity, you should cherish it. I'll show you where her stuff is in the basement. But do try not to get locked in there, or even discovered in there, will you, Kate? We don't want to worry the old boys unnecessarily."

Harriet led Kate to the basement, an area with which she had, through her weekly seminar, become somewhat familiar. Harriet, who appeared, like a medieval chatelaine, to have all the household keys dangling from her belt, opened a small storage room, waved a welcoming hand, and pulled the string to turn on the light. "All yours," she said. "Good luck. Just bang the door shut when you leave."

Kate settled down to her task; she pulled out a box and sat on it while examining the other boxes by the light of the single bulb dangling from the ceiling. Almost all the boxes contained books, and files removed from their file drawers—doubtless the file cabinet itself was passed on to someone else. Kate hoped, shamelessly, that among the law books would be a novel that Nellie had marked with pinpricks to indicate a code contrived to reveal the nefarious secrets she had uncovered about Schuyler. There was no novel. The files all contained class schedules, student papers, student records —at least up to the last year of her life. The most recent ones had been removed so that her orphaned students might be granted a grade, or so Kate surmised. Kate reproved herself for her idiotic expectations. Nellie had not known she would die; she had not left clues to her murderer, if any. If she had learned anything untoward about the school, she had not recorded it, or if she had recorded it, someone had seen to its removal.

Kate moved off her box and, sitting back on her heels, turned over its contents. More papers relating to law—Nellie had taught

Contracts—and a few letters addressed to her. This box, then, held the contents of Nellie's desk. The letters were all academic, the sort Kate regularly received at her university, different content, same themes. Nellie had had a desk set, and it was here: a blotter, left over from the days when people actually wrote with fountain pens, a leather letter holder that matched, and a picture frame. The picture was of Nellie—Kate had seen her picture in an old catalog of Schuyler Law—and a man, standing with his arm around her shoulder, both of them laughing. Carefully, Kate removed the picture from the frame, but there was nothing written on the back; carefully, she reinserted it in the frame. Kate would have to find out who he was.

But she had no hope that anything would come of this information. You're off on a wild-goose chase, she told herself; pondering a mare's nest, grasping at straws. Nellie may have known New York, Kate and many others knew New York, its traffic dangers included, but that didn't mean that one couldn't be killed by a truck. Probably Nellie's fall under the truck's wheels was as unintended as the truck driver's crushing her. Your detective whiskers are quivering, Kate told herself, and they are picking up nothing, because nothing is in the wind.

She turned out the light, allowed the door to slam behind her, and headed for home. She had taken the picture with her, still in its frame that matched the blotter and letter holder, promising Nellie to return it to the storeroom if it proved to lead nowhere.

Once home, she called Blair's apartment; he had not yet returned; she left a message asking him to call her, and wondered if this was wise. Wise or not, she had to decide either to forget Nellie or to follow up the man in this picture, if Blair knew who he was.

It was some hours later that Blair returned her call. She had wondered how much to tell him about how she had acquired the picture, and ended, as she usually did end, with the truth. He listened to her account of the storage room and its disappointing contents with some amusement, conveyed by the intermittent chuckle.

"It was a characteristic Schuyler cleanup," Blair said. "As it happens, I was there at my own insistence when the cleaning staff cleared out her office. I was still angry about her death, and in pain. They dumped her belongings into boxes—the ones you found, no doubt—and left everything else that belonged to the school right there—the furniture, the computer, the bookshelves. She had a picture on the wall, and I offered to call her parents to ask if they wanted it. They didn't; it was a reproduction of Mary Cassatt's *The Boating Party*."

"It's in your office now," Kate said. "I noticed it."

"Yes. I've pondered it a good deal. It says a great deal about family life, that picture—Nellie mentioned it to me. The baby's eyes are on the man, the woman's eyes are on the man and the baby, the man's eyes are on his rowing, or perhaps the shore. Nellie was also impressed with the composition; anyway, I kept it as a memento from her."

"There was a picture on her desk," Kate said, not mentioning that she had borrowed it. "At least, I assume it was; the frame matches her desk blotter. It's a picture of her with a man. Do you know who he is, or was?"

"He is, or was, her brother. They were incredibly close all their lives, or so I gathered from Nellie. It quite amazed me, because I have a sister and we are distantly polite with wholly different interests. Why?"

"I'd like to talk to him. Do you know where he lives?"

"Hold on. I have to think. He's a poet, and gives courses in various universities—that's how he supports himself. But I seem to remember he had a more or less permanent position teaching somewhere in the Midwest. Damn."

"Was his name Rosenbusch, too?"

"Yes. And I can't come up with his first name either. I'll ask myself tonight when going to sleep, and the answer may be there when I wake up. That sometimes happens. I'll let you know when it comes to me, but if you know any poets, they may be more help than I can be."

"Thanks, Blair."

"You know, Kate, she may not have been more than distracted when she went under that truck. I don't think the brother ought to be—"

"Trust me for that," Kate said. If I ever find him, she reminded herself, hanging up the phone.

Blair's nighttime directions to his unconscious proved disappointing. Kate had been to graduate school with a couple of male poets, men who had persevered in their craft, not trying to mount the academic ladder but picking up what teaching jobs they could here and there. She called them in the hope that one of them might have heard of poet Rosenbusch. It was, of course, not easy to locate her poet friends, whose lives were peripatetic by definition, and it was some days before she tracked one of them down. He, however, was unexpectedly helpful.

"Of course I know Rosie," he bellowed happily over the phone, after he and Kate had exchanged the usual questions and answers. "Good poet. He lives in New Hampshire. I'll try to dig up his address and get back to you. If it's poetry you want, can't I help?"

"If it were, you could," Kate said. "Do try to find the address or the phone number, will you? It's rather important."

"I'm off now on the search," he said. "I suppose you have one of those beastly machines on which I can leave a message?"

"I have." She gave him the number.

"When I next come to New York, I expect to be given a lavish dinner at one of those snooty restaurants."

"For you, anything," Kate promised. "Even a snooty restaurant."

Later that day Kate's machine recorded poet Rosenbusch's address but not his phone number. "I tried information," the machine repeated, "but it's unlisted. Smart fellow. I hope you have some powerful pull with the phone company. Is there a restaurant called Luchese?"

Neither the phone company nor Reed, when she recruited him to help, could wrest the phone number of poet Rosenbusch (whose first name was Charles) from the telephone company. Kate was hot on the trail, for no reason she could have logically explained, but even she refused to fabricate a family emergency in order to get his number. He had had enough of a family emergency already.

"I'll have to go to see him and hope he's home," Kate said.

Reed groaned. "He probably won't be there, and if he is, he probably won't want to talk to you. I wouldn't want to talk to you if my sister had recently died that way, if I had a sister."

"You might," Kate said. "Sometimes it's easier to talk to a stranger about your feelings and troubles."

"That is a cliché I have always considered spurious," Reed said.

"Anyway," Kate said. "I'm going. I'll fly to Boston and rent a car. New Hampshire, at least his part, is quite near. I will get a sense of accomplishment even if I accomplish nothing."

"I hope your battery dies, you get caught in a snowdrift, and are only rescued on the point of starvation," Reed said.

"No, you don't," Kate said. "You hope I find him, because you know I want to, however irrational the desire."

"Okay, then, but be careful," Reed said when she left that weekend for the airport.

6

Who owns him? she wondered helplessly.
Who writes his lines and gives him his directions?

—JOHN LE CARRÉ
THE LITTLE DRUMMER GIRL

Charles Rosenbusch lived in a small house that faced on the square of a small New Hampshire village. There was a church, a graveyard, a common, and one or two other houses. Kate knocked at the door of the wrong house before having the right one pointed out to her. Rosenbusch did not respond to a knock on his front door, and Kate finally trailed around to the back to find him, or at least a man, clearing bushes at the edge of his back field.

"I'm looking for Charles Rosenbusch," Kate called out, after her hello had made him raise his head. He turned back to his bushes. "It's about your sister, Nellie," Kate added. She began to feel that she was making a fool of herself, and had come on a mindless excursion; if she had had a rational reason, it seemed to be escaping her now. Really, she should listen to Reed when contemplating this sort of idiocy.

But Rosenbusch had dropped the tools with which he had been attacking the undergrowth, and walked toward her.

"You knew Nellie?" he asked.

"I'm grappling with her memory and her death," Kate said. "Could I take a moment to explain?"

"You didn't know her." It was a statement.

"Give me ten minutes to explain," Kate said. "Standing right here. We'll synchronize our watches. If in ten minutes you say go, I'll go."

He took her at her word, literally, glancing at his watch as she glanced at hers. There was no need to synchronize them; ten minutes is ten minutes. I've seen too many war movies, Kate told herself. They stood, perhaps three feet apart, his defensive stance daring her to interest him.

"I am teaching at Schuyler Law School this semester; I'm a professor of literature, on leave from my regular job, teaching a course on law and literature with Blair Whitson. He was a friend of Nellie's. Blair and I have questions about Nellie's death. There is little chance of proving anything, one way or the other, but we would like to know more about Nellie, for our own sakes, and because something she knew may help us to bring those who tormented her—and she was tormented—to justice, if not for her murder, at least for something. You are the only person who may be able to tell us something about her. I want to know if you saw her in the months before her death, and if she told you anything that might be of use to us in learning what was on her mind toward the end of her life."

"Did you talk to our parents? Is that how you heard of me?"

"No. I found a picture of you and Nellie among her belongings. They are in a storeroom, since apparently neither you nor your parents wanted them. Blair knew it was you in the picture. I found out your address from a poet friend of mine." And Kate named him.

Kate paused, though her ten minutes were not even half used up. Rosenbusch seemed to make up his mind.

"You better come in," he said. "What's your name, by the way?"

"Kate Fansler."

"Okay, Kate. Let's talk awhile. My name's Charles, but these days everybody calls me Rosie."

He led the way into the house through the back door; past the mud room, they entered a large sunny kitchen, made to seem even sunnier by the yellow floor and chintz chairs before the fireplace opposite the kitchen's business end.

I am destined to talk in kitchens, Kate thought.

He sat down in one chair and pointed her to a chair opposite. "How can I help?" he said. Kate remembered that he had been smiling in the picture, laughing even, with his arm around Nellie. Now he seemed somber enough to make that laughter implausible.

"Tell me what Nellie talked about during the time she was at Schuyler Law; anything connected with the school or its inhabitants. Anything, no matter how inconsequential it seems to you."

"We talked of everything; we always did. I might as well give you the picture of our relationship, our love. I'm glad to see you don't cringe at the word *love* between a brother and a sister. We're not talking Wagner here, or youthful familial passions. We simply liked and loved each other. I've often thought," he added, growing pensive—his eyes had never been directly on Kate—"that the brother-and-sister bond has been ignored by psychologists and novelists and others of that ilk. Freud got them so caught up in the damned Oedipus complex that no other attachment seemed equally compelling. Stupid, really."

"Were you twins?"

"I told you, no Wagner. I was eighteen months older; eighteen months in which I sometimes think I was waiting for her, waiting for her to be my friend and my companion against the parents. Oh, don't get any idea that they were cruel or mean or other than perfectly good middle-class parents. They were just dull, and full of conventional ideas, and wanting for us what, as they often said, any parents want for their boy and girl. The boy to make a nice living, the girl to marry a nice man. They argued with each other, of course, in a folie à deux that is probably emblematic of most marriages. Nellie and I simply had a different life."

"Did she call you Rosie?" Kate asked after a longish pause, for something to say.

"She called me Charles. I called her Nellie because the parents called her Elinor, her name. Someone told her that Nellie was

80

short for Elinor, and we latched on to that. So," he added after a moment, "if you want to know did we talk of everything together, the answer is yes, we did, to the very end."

Kate waited. He would get to Schuyler. Her mouth was dry, but no drink seemed in the offing. She would have rather liked a cup of tea or, lacking that, a drink of water. But she feared to interrupt his speech and his memories.

"She was happy when she got the job at Schuyler," he said. "She knew it wasn't a great law school, or even a good one, but she liked the fact that some of the students, particularly the women, were older and serious and putting a lot on the line to be there, unlike most of the kids at the fancier places. Also, she wanted to be in New York, something I never understood. She wasn't into isolation, the way I am; she wasn't solitary by nature. We met often—she'd come here for the weekend, or we'd meet somewhere outside New York; I hate the city—and we talked on the telephone a lot. I always sent her my poems."

"I tried to buy them," Kate said. "In the end I found them in the library. If you know where I could get a copy, I'd be grateful. I like your poems."

"What do you like about them?" he asked, suspicious.

"You have a voice," she said. "I like to hear the poet's voice in poems. Is that old-fashioned?"

"Not by me. Nellie said that—you have a voice. Funny; and you never knew her."

"No. Yet when Blair speaks of her, I get a sense of what she was like, of what she was after."

"Blair was nice to her. At first I thought he was just another man she was carrying on with, but he really did seem to understand what she was up against. He did support her; of course, there wasn't anybody else except the students, and she was there for them, not them for her. What was it you wanted to know about exactly?"

"Anything about Schuyler, about her time there—her impressions, her suspicions, her reactions, her plans. Anything at all that was connected to the law school."

"She was appalled at first, and then angry. I don't think she had really faced what men like those in the faculty were like. Nellie really believed that if you treated people with honor, they recognized that and honored you in return. It may sound naive, but nothing in her life up to then had dislodged that faith. Of course she had met some shits, but if she was working with people anywhere, they always seemed to recognize her—well, her sincerity, I guess, and her integrity. That sounds a fancy way to put it, but that's what she had and that's what she thought would be perceived. Not at Schuyler, not a chance. I pointed out that people without integrity couldn't recognize it; liars can never trust anyone, that stands to reason. By the time she saw what they were like, the men on that faculty, she became unhappy, and then angry. I told her to get out, but she stayed through her tenure fight, Blair was great about that, and then I really thought she might leave, she had some feelers out." He paused, as though making up his mind. "It was then," he finally said, "that she began to suspect they were not only reactionaries, but mean reactionaries."

"Isn't that a tautology?"

"Not necessarily. I don't suppose reactionaries are any meaner to their nearest and dearest than anyone else. It's the way they treat people who are out of the loop that marks them as mean. And Nellie was certainly out of the loop."

"Far enough out to be killed?" Kate asked. He seemed a man who didn't mind direct speech, and he certainly seemed a man who wasn't likely to want to sit around chatting all day.

"You mean, did they push her under that truck? Is that what you suspect?"

"It seems to be a possible suspicion, at least to those who knew and liked her. And to the police, who went so far as to check alibis, which were, incidentally, notably lacking."

"That was before they found out about her health. I had to tell them. Look, Kate, I know you came up here to do what you could for Nellie, now that she's dead. And you came to the right person; your instincts can't be faulted. I've lost the person who meant the most to me, who always meant the most to me, and I'm hoping that solitude, hard physical work, and poems that let me speak of my mourning will see me out of this. I'd love to pin her death on those bastards, but the fact is she just blacked out and fell in front of that truck. I pity the poor driver, I really do."

"Blacked out?"

"Need we go into the medical details? She had an affliction, an illness, it got worse rather than better, but she handled it with medication and determination. Its most dangerous symptom was that she would black out, lose consciousness, and, inevitably, fall. She'd got that symptom under control, or the doctors had, but there's no doubt she blacked out and fell in front of that truck. I'm damn sure the stress those men caused her led to an intensification of her illness and thus to her death, but I don't think we can call it murder, if that's what you're after."

"I see," Kate said, feeling a fool, rushing off in all directions like Nancy Drew to prove murder, when all she could prove there was what was equally evident in New York: the faculty of Schuyler Law were, on the whole, an unattractive bunch—well, a bunch of mediocre shits, she thought, taking refuge in strong language. So he's here trying to put his life together, and I'm asking fool questions.

He seemed to sense her mood. "Don't feel bad about coming here," he said. "I'm glad for a chance to talk about Nellie. I know I've got to find some center for my life, but at the moment I just try to keep the terrors at bay. And thank you for not asking if I was married, or living here alone, or what? Are you married?"

"Yes," Kate said.

"You don't wear a ring. Nellie always said she wouldn't wear a ring either, if she married."

"I don't wear a ring, use his name, or depend upon him financially. He's a lawyer, by the way, but not a neoconservative, and this semester he's actually doing a clinic for Schuyler Law, where I teach law and literature with Blair."

"What kind of clinic? Nellie said they didn't have clinics at Schuyler."

"They didn't have real clinics, so to speak. They had synthetic clinics, which are useful, but don't help people or plunge the students into actual legal situations. Reed's clinic is working with prisoners who want to contest their cases, or who are being held in prison improperly, or are being mistreated there."

"Nellie worried about someone in prison, the wife of one of the law professors. She'd met her only once, I think, but said her case should be retried because the lawyer she had at the time hadn't known of some syndrome."

"The battered woman syndrome. One of the law professors mentioned her to me at their semiannual reception; his view was that she'd murdered his colleague and friend, and deserved to be in jail, if not on death row."

"That's the woman, I guess. What's the battered woman syndrome, or don't I want to know?"

"As I understand it, which doesn't say much for my defining it properly, it has to do with the fact that self-defense can be considered a justification for murder if the murderer felt her life in danger at the moment she struck. You pull a gun on me and I, faster on the draw, shoot you before you shoot me."

"I see you spent your youth watching Western movies," he said. Kate smiled. It was the first remotely relaxed comment he had made.

"With battered women, however," she continued, "they wait until the batterer is asleep or watching television or chatting with someone at a bar. Then they kill him. To defend such a woman against a charge of outright murder, the law has tried to explain that a battered woman doesn't dare protect herself at the moment she is being battered; if she has the courage at all to protect herself, she will wait until the man is at his least dangerous."

"I get it. Well, Nellie hoped someone could reopen this woman's case, so maybe if you can get your husband's clinic to do that, you won't have dragged yourself all the way to New Hampshire in vain."

Kate understood that the conversation was over. She rose, and he rose with her.

"Thank you for talking to me," she said.

"Thank you for caring about Nellie even though you never met her, for coming all this way, and for talking to me straight without either questions or advice. I'm sorry you didn't know Nellie; you would have liked each other."

As they moved toward the door, the front door this time, he said, "Wait a minute," and vanished into a room. He reappeared with a book. "My poems. Thank you for going to some trouble to read them."

"Thank you," Kate said, meaning it.

When she was in the car, she opened the book of poems, hoping he had at least signed it. He had done more than that. *For Kate*, he had written, *who cared about Nellie and doesn't ask too many questions*.

Kate closed the book with, she was surprised to realize, intense emotion. She had to wait for tears to recede from her eyes before she was able to drive away.

Kate was late getting home and tired from the drive to the airport, the plane trip, the drive from the New York airport, and the simultaneous sense of being glad to have met Rosie, brave in his grief, and foolish in having turned a terrible accident into murder because she thought some men capable of murder. She and Reed sat with their drinks; Kate was glad to be silent for a while beside him; she would tell him about the visit to Rosie, but not yet. She had to get used to it in her mind first. What she was used to in her mind, however, was the dreariness of Schuyler Law.

"I know you will do good with your clinic, and maybe my spouting literature in counterpoint to law will give someone an idea, but I can't help wondering why we had to do all this in so crummy a law school. Why did we have to end up in such a depressing place? Surely most other law schools are a lot better. Please say they are."

"It's pretty astonishing, Kate," Reed said. "It started me looking around my own law school. And then there's Harvard. Where they claim that the reason they haven't got a tenured black woman is because there simply isn't one good enough for Harvard. Meaning, freely translated, she doesn't teach law the way they think law should be taught. And speaking of Harvard, I've brought you a book to read."

"Ah, the intellectual's solution to everything. What book is it?"

"You sneer at books! You must be tired. You know as well as I that they have changed the world and may be all that can."

"Sorry, Reed. I'm feeling foolish, and when I feel foolish I get argumentative; foolishly, of course. What book have you brought me?"

"It's about the Harvard Law School, and no, it's not the one by Scott Turow. It's called *Broken Contract*, by a guy named Kahlenberg.[1] If you don't want to read it and be plunged into further dismay, I'll tell you its main point. Public service, the ideal with which most Harvard Law students and, one supposes, students at other like institutions, enter the study of law, is abandoned by these students in large numbers. Partly it's money; corporate law offers huge salaries compared with public service law, and many law students have large loans to pay back. Partly it's that Harvard Law cooperates with corporate law firms, who are their wealthiest alumni and contributors, in directing the students that way. Mostly, however, it's that students early discover that power does not lie in public service; such jobs rarely lead to political appointments, let alone the good life, elegant working conditions, and a place in the power loop. Harvard Law School, like the others in the same rank, preach service but make sure their graduates are not deluded by the sermons."

"The author of this book seems to have convinced you," Kate said. "Maybe he's wrong, or has an ax to grind, or just hates Harvard, a not uncommon emotion."

"Maybe. But he quotes a speech from the then-president of Har-

[1] Richard D. Kahlenberg, *Broken Contract: A Memoir of Harvard Law School.* Faber and Faber, 1992.

vard, Derek Bok. Ten years earlier, in the first Reagan years, Bok had given a speech deploring the rush to corporate law. He expressed regret at how the brightest students had diverted their talents to 'pursuits that often add little to the growth of the economy, the pursuit of culture, or the enhancement of the human spirit.' The author calls Bok 'the master of inconsistency,' because when it came time to appoint a new dean of the law school, which was divided between the liberals and the neoconservatives, Bok threw his weight behind the ultraconservative candidate for dean, a leading spokesman for the right. As a result, gifts to the law school soared by sixty-four percent."

"Schuyler Law," Kate said, after a pause, and in rather hopeless tones, "is not Harvard Law. There isn't and never was any 'left' there at all."

"There's you and Blair and me, and Bobby helping me. Have a little gumption, Kate, please. You don't usually become quite this damp and hopeless."

"Reed, there's a battered woman in your prison named Betty Osborne. I mentioned her after that wonderful faculty reception. She's the one who shot her husband, a law professor from Schuyler, because he was beating her. Couldn't you use the battered woman syndrome to get her a retrial?"

"Kate, the prisoners have to request our help. We can't go in and recruit them; that's not how it works. What brought her to mind all of a sudden?"

"Nellie's brother. He mentioned that Nellie had been concerned about her. Please try and do something. If she will let you help her, it may be the only result of my impulsive trip to New Hampshire."

"You got a book of poems."

"So I did."

"Kate, if you will cheer up, I'll promise to have a word with Betty Osborne. I can't make her request our help, but I can let her know we're there. It's a bit irregular, but I'll do it. On one condition: that you cheer up, right now. At least, pretend to cheer up and stop me worrying about you. I don't want to go back to thinking you're in a phase, as your mother said."

"It's a bargain, Reed. I don't feel much like talking cheerful. Could we try being cheerful in bed?"

"I thought you'd never ask," Reed said, glad to make her smile.

7

*Please don't ever imagine you'll be unscathed by the methods
you use. The end may justify the means—if it wasn't
supposed to, I dare say you wouldn't be here. But there's a
price to pay, and the price does tend to be oneself.*

—JOHN LE CARRÉ
THE SECRET PILGRIM

Kate returned to Schuyler for her seminar the next day, reassured by Reed's promise to learn what he could from Betty Osborne. She reported to Harriet the substance of her New Hampshire visit: Nellie had not been killed. Harriet listened, in the women's room, to Kate's account, and seemed unimpressed.

"No doubt the brother's right," she said, "technically speaking. They killed her all the same, the bastards. Why is it that men with retrograde opinions have no manners? They come into the secretaries' room and order me and the other women around. Sometimes they come in, looking for a fellow conspirator, and if he's not there they say, 'Oh, there's no one here.' I've trained the women to sing out in unison, 'There's somebody here; there's a bunny rabbit underneath the radiator.' It's had a surprisingly good effect."

"Men like these," Kate said, "have good manners to women they consider their social equals. They're only rude to women over whom they have power. That's the explanation of most sexual harassment, in case you hadn't noticed."

"Of course I've noticed. At least I've been able to maintain an atmosphere of no bottom smacking or cheek pinching in my secretaries' room. 'Go home and pat your wife,' I say to them. Really, Kate, there's been a change. They creep in the door now, and behave like lambs once inside. They have definitely decided not to mess with me. And they don't want to be rid of me, because I get the work done. This is known as having them by the short and curlies: hands and hats off, boys, I say."

Kate, considerably cheered by Harriet's grip on things, went down to the seminar room where Blair was waiting. Blair, too, seemed to feel that things were looking up. A good deal of what Kate and he had been saying seemed, suddenly, to have taken root. As a result, instead of discussing legal and literary treatments of rape, Kate and Blair found themselves this afternoon being questioned about the law school itself.

While they were still, at the beginning of the seminar, parrying questions and trying to decide without the benefit of consultation how to deal with this new openness, a male student strode to the door of the classroom, locked it with a key he had with him, and stood facing the class.

"No one leaves till I say so," he ordered, "and no one telephones." He glared at the young woman who had had the phone on the last occasion. Blair looked at Kate and both simultaneously recognized that the last attempt to incarcerate the class had gone awry, and this student, or whoever had planned it, had seen the trick fail. The call to the police had gone out too fast. This time the student was better prepared; he had decided or been ordered to lock the door himself, and he had done so. He now faced Blair in a confrontational stance that was, Kate realized, what was meant by squaring off.

"I've had enough of your goddamn bullshit," the young man said to Blair, "and I'm going to show you how real men behave. If there's one thing I hate worse than fags, it's straight men who let women tell them what to do." And he launched himself at Blair, punching him first in the stomach and then, as Blair bent over in pain, in the face. Kate and everyone else in the room stood as though paralyzed. In the lengthy moment it took Blair to collapse on the floor and the student to leap on him, Kate realized that outside of movies and television, she had never seen any men she knew personally fighting. The whole thing resembled a staged fight for a characteristically violent film of the day, providing guns and knives had been, for some eccentric reason of plot, avoided. All this was the thought of a second: she was uncertain what to do.

The students in the class, however, if less literarily inclined, were more practical. One of the young women picked up a chair, hoisted it above her head, and brought it down on the back of Blair's assailant. Obviously, a young woman who worked out, which Kate did not. Nonetheless, grasping the strategy, she and others grabbed chairs and began shoving them onto the belligerent student, still on top of Blair. The effect was confused but effective; the student rolled away from the chairs, and Blair grabbed him.

In the extraordinary (to Kate) manner of the indestructible men in films, Blair started punching the student, who was considerably taller and heavier, until the student, in his turn, was lying on the floor with Blair hovering over him, waiting for him to get up. At that moment Kate remembered the student's first name, which was Jake. (Blair had insisted on running the class on a first-name basis, and Kate never did learn which last name went with whom until almost the end of the semester.)

Blair, tired of hovering, pulled Jake to his feet and slammed him against the wall, where he held him up with one hand, while threatening him with the other, should he move. Jake seemed either worn-out, or biding his time. "What the fuck do you think you're doing?" Blair asked, shaking him as though a reasonable explanation might just possibly fall out.

"I've been taping this bullshit class," Jake said, shaking himself loose but carefully not suggesting any further violence. "I've been listening to all this propaganda, cases where guys rape girls because the damn girls can't make up their minds even when your balls are blue. And what the hell are girls for anyway? You people, you and this crazy dame, are polluting the whole atmosphere of this law school and of the country, and I intend to put a stop to it. That's what the fuck I'm doing."

"Give me the key," Blair said, holding out his hand.

After a moment's consideration, Jake handed it over, hatred oozing from him like sweat. Blair unlocked the door, but did not open it; he pocketed the key.

"How many of you knew that this guy was taping the class?" he asked. He motioned Kate to the seat next to him and sat down. Jake leaned against a wall. "Lean over there," Blair said to him, pointing to the farther wall. "I want to be able to see you. Or sit down, if that position is compatible with your profound dignity. But keep your hands on the table."

Jake sat down, reached into his pocket as Blair rose menacingly to his feet, and then slid the tape recorder across the table toward Blair. "You can keep this tape," he said. "I have plenty of others. With copies." He sneered.

Blair removed the tape and put the recorder in his jacket pocket. "I'll return it when this class is over," he said. "Don't forget to ask me for it. Now, as I was saying, how many of you knew this class was being taped?"

For a time there was silence, long enough for Kate to wonder what Blair would do next—she herself hadn't, she realized, the least idea of what to do—when a young woman spoke up.

"I knew," she said. "I encouraged him. He seemed to be a real guy, not like the other so-called men in the class— well, that's what I thought then," she added, looking around apologetically. "I mean, Jake was going with a friend of mine and she thought it was a great idea. I'm not so sure I still think so. Anyway, I'd started reading up on the law on taping without permission. It's complicated, but I thought one's motives should come into it. I mean, you know, well, I didn't think Jake would want me to tape some of his conversations about this class. Would you, Jake?" she added, turning toward him. Jake started to snarl something, and then stopped.

"What really got to me," the young woman, whose name was Tilly, went on, "was that he somehow got hold of a picture of Kate,

Professor Fansler, and attached it to one of the worst kind of centerfolds from *Hustler,* or some such porn magazine. He passed it around, and everyone sort of laughed at first, and then some of us began to wonder if we'd really like someone to do that to us, and if it was really fair. I mean, Kate never pretended to be a sex object, did she? It seemed like taking Jake's head and putting it on the picture of a guy with a tiny little prick, if you know what I mean."

Smiles around the table indicated that they knew what she meant. Neither Kate nor Blair smiled. It all seemed far more crude and violent and intrusive than anything they had imagined possible in a classroom.

"Did Jake show this composite centerfold to anyone on the faculty?" Kate asked. The women around the table exchanged glances. "I take it," Kate said, "that silence means consent. Why is it I'm so certain the faculty found it screamingly funny?"

Blair looked at his watch and exchanged a glance with Kate, who looked at hers and nodded. "We'll call this class over for today," he said. "If anyone tries again to lock that door or any door with me on the other side of it, I promise you your future in any kind of law practice will become singularly difficult. Everybody out."

They left the room slowly, as though sensing that the situation had not been satisfactorily resolved, as indeed it hadn't. When they were gone, Kate and Blair, still seated, looked at each other and, almost simultaneously, sighed.

"I'm sorry you had to put up with that," Blair said. "You're taking it with remarkable equanimity. You *are* all right, aren't you, Kate?"

She was silent for a moment. "I am all right, thank you. And I find I'm wondering why. I mean, that's a pretty brutal thing to do to any woman. But the mean boys in *Hustler* and *Playboy* have been playing that trick for a long time now. And a woman-professor friend of mine even had the same treatment, far more skillfully carried out, from a right-wing journal. The idea isn't shocking anymore; it's on a par with being told that all feminists hate men and won't wear makeup. I don't imagine this little job was done very skillfully. It isn't the picture, Blair, it's the hatred and the fear. The degree to which some men are threatened by feminism. But it doesn't make me fearful and vulnerable anymore, it just makes me first angry, and then thoughtful—wondering what the threat really is."

"That's simple." He got up and stood behind her chair, putting his arms over hers and then massaging the back of her neck and shoulders. "They're afraid that their natural and unquestioned position at the top of the ladder is becoming less secure. The ladder's shaking, and they are in grave danger of falling off the top."

"You don't seem worried."

"Maybe because I don't find the top as appealing as some. I've decided I don't care a great deal for the guys who make it up there."

"You sound like Harriet," Kate said, getting up. "Thanks for the massage; I *was* tense."

"Better than sounding like our dean," he said. "Let's go." They walked together back to Blair's office, where, seated on opposite sides of the desk, they smiled at each other.

"I didn't know you could fight like that," Kate said. "Do all men do that? I've spent so much time with literary types that I never noticed, and missed out on all the action. I've never seen Reed hit anyone."

"I was a street kid long ago," Blair said, "and I've stayed in shape. He hit me in the stomach, which I wasn't ready for, but I had hardened those muscles, almost automatically, in anticipation. I'm what they call an A-type, so I've had to learn to be ready for what comes."

"An A-type," Kate repeated. "You mean the sort who can't stand waiting on line, and finishes everybody's sentences, and fights over parking spaces—that kind of A-type?"

"More or less," Blair said. "Except, as you may have noticed, I've tried to stop finishing people's sentences, at least most of the time. The question is, what in hell are we going to do about Jake?"

"I haven't an idea in the world, at least not at this moment,"

94

Kate said. She stood up, anxious to get away from all this and especially from the excruciating fact that this revolting masculine display had made Blair sharply, noticeably attractive. I'm responding to cavemen, she thought; What the hell is the matter with me? This damn place is driving me bonkers, that's what it is, and turning me into someone who *ought* to want to be in a centerfold. Well, anyway, able to respond to the sort of man who responds to centerfolds? Oh, shit, as Jake would say.

"I think we should make sure that guy's actions do not go unreported to his potential employers," Blair said. "I mean, if they think he acted in a manly and proper fashion, they're free to hire him, and good luck. But other types should be warned."

"I don't know," Kate said. "I think he did us a favor, really. He's turned some of the students around more effectively than we might have done without his help. I think he's the sort who's his own worst enemy."

"That's because he didn't punch you in the gut," Blair said. "Not that I'd put it past him. The problem is—"

There was a knock on the door, and whatever Blair's problem was remained unexpressed. He went to the door and admitted a woman Kate recognized as Bobby, Reed's assistant director of the clinic.

"Hi," she said. "Sorry to intrude." Kate introduced her to Blair. "Nice to meet you. I've come to waft Kate off to Staten Island. You don't mind if I call you Kate, do you? I don't want to presume on one dinner and a working relationship with your husband."

"You're not presuming. Why should I go to Staten Island?"

"Because Betty Osborne has agreed to see you, and Reed thinks it ought to be this afternoon. She could ask for you through regular channels, and you'd get a visitor's pass, but Reed thought maybe we better strike while the iron was hot. So I'm to drive you out there. If you want to call Reed at home, he'll explain. But hurry, he won't be there long."

Kate stared at Bobby for a worried moment; then she crossed the room to the telephone.

"It's me," she said when Reed picked up. "You're supposed to tell me why I have to leave for Staten Island this very minute."

"Betty Osborne asked to see you. We talked our way into seeing her, Bobby and I, when we were out there this morning with some of the students. We managed to arrange for the coordinator to let you see her this afternoon. He won't be there tomorrow, and I don't know when else. We've got to grab this opportunity, Kate. They could well change their minds, and insist on your applying as a regular visitor through the proper channels. I told them you'd be there this afternoon."

"Can't you come with me?"

"I can't, Kate. Didn't Bobby tell you? I have to go to court with a student. Bobby will go with you; she knows the way, and the drill, all that. She's got a prison ID for you to wear."

"Am I supposed to be a lawyer?"

"Of course not. The ID just means you're connected with a properly registered lawyer—me—and with Bobby, who they know is working with me. Okay then?"

"Okay then," Kate said. "But just tell me, why did she ask for me?"

"She's heard of you. Ask Bobby. I've got to go. See you at home."

Kate turned to Bobby. "All right," she said. "I'll make a pit stop first. How do we go?"

"I've got a car. We take the Verrazano Bridge."

"You mean I don't even get a ferry ride?"

"It's faster. Come on, Kate. We said you'd be there by four-thirty at the latest."

"Not till you tell me why me?"

"She was a graduate student in English, at your university, I think. She seems to want to talk to a literary type. Maybe all she wants is to argue with you about the English novel. Come on, Kate!"

Kate looked at Blair, who shrugged his shoulders. "Talk to you

96

later," he said. Kate picked up her bag and marched down the hall to the women's room.

"Don't take forever," Bobby said.

Kate wanted to stick out her tongue at her, but decided that Bobby's eagerness was on Betty Osborne's behalf, no rudeness to Kate intended.

8

So it went on, one argument predicating another, until the only logic was the fiction, and the fiction was a web that enmeshed everyone who tried to sweep it away.

—JOHN LE CARRÉ
THE LITTLE DRUMMER GIRL

Once they were away in the car and free of the worst of the traffic in lower Manhattan, Kate looked at Bobby, intent on her driving. "I still don't understand why we have to go today, right off the bat like this. Why wouldn't tomorrow do?"

"You don't understand how it works," Bobby said.

"Of course I don't understand. I also don't understand how the law school works, how any law school works. God only knows what I'm doing there, or here with you, for that matter."

"Sorry," Bobby said, glancing over for a moment at Kate. "You see, we regularly visit the prison on Wednesday afternoons. The people there have to be notified of the clients we wish to see by noon of the Monday preceding our visit. You can't just add names. Getting you in there this afternoon took a lot of special pleading. It's a favor to Reed, who really saw the chance to learn something about this woman, and pulled a lot of levers to make it possible for you to see her right away. I understand he did this because you particularly asked him to. That's why all the hurry. I'm sorry if I was too pressuring about it."

They rode in silence for a bit, over the traffic-clogged routes to the bridge. It never failed to amaze Kate, the few times she ventured out of Manhattan, through Queens to the airports or, today, through Brooklyn, how the roads were always jammed, no matter what the hour, and how there always seemed to be an accident of some sort to add to the congestion. Bobby, like Kate and Reed, drove a standard shift, so that she had continually to change gears on this start-and-stop trip, grunting with impatience at each plunge of the clutch.

"Why don't you talk, Bobby?" Kate said. "It beats sitting here seething at the traffic, as though it were a watched pot that wouldn't boil."

Bobby, changing lanes, said nothing. Even in the new lane, which now stopped moving just as the old one had, she still said nothing.

"What do you know about this woman I'm going to see?" Kate asked. It seemed a reasonable question.

"No more than you do. She shot her husband; she got the gun from someone. I'm sure she'll tell you all about it. All she said was that she wanted to talk to you. We haven't even got the papers yet, because we haven't got her case. Maybe you can arrange that—to get her to ask for Reed to manage her appeal, I mean. Surely you can manage that."

They reentered the zone of silence. Kate decided, as they approached it, that she had never before been across the Verrazano Bridge. Well, who, after all, did she know on Staten Island? In her extreme youth, she had ridden on the ferry, but only for the ride. It occurred to Kate, not for the first time, that she knew remarkably little beyond Manhattan about New York City. But, she comforted herself, she knew more than the city's employees, policemen, firemen, sanitation workers, bus drivers, most of whom lived somewhere beyond the city limits, even in New Jersey. Policemen in Japan, she had read, always lived in the district they policed. What interesting facts one picked up and remembered in strange boroughs.

After a time Kate decided to break the silence. She turned a bit in her seat to face Bobby more directly.

"You've fallen in love with Reed, haven't you?" she asked, as gently as she could. "I've always thought the phrase *fallen in love* particularly apposite. I mean, that's what happens, isn't it? One minute we're on firm ground, the next minute we're in a free fall."

Bobby turned to look at her so steadily that Kate grabbed the handle just above the door. "Watch it," she said. "However you may feel at the moment, nothing will be solved by our crashing into something on the Verrazano Bridge. Think of the traffic. Think of the prisoners. Think of that dreadful law school."

"I couldn't help it," Bobby said. "He doesn't know, please believe me. It's just my craziness."

"I would be very surprised if he didn't know," Kate said. "But he will never let you or even himself face the fact. That's the male way of dealing with things, and I have to admit, reluctantly, that from time to time it works."

"You don't mind. Not that you have anything to worry about . . ."

"Let's say I'm not exactly in any position to mind."

"What do you mean?"

"I don't know what I mean," Kate said. "Reed is very attractive and very lovable. Is it hard, working with him every day?"

"It isn't every day, it's just twice a week; once when we go to the prison, and once in the office when he comes in to look things over. Mostly, I'm there keeping the records, answering the phone, checking up to see the students come in at least once a day to get messages and see how their cases are going."

"Bobby," Kate said, sighing. "Please keep your eyes on the road. You don't have to look at me, just listen. Help Reed to get on with his clinic, and it will pass, I promise. Just don't act on any of these obsessions when you're working with him, and by the end of this semester a lot of this will be over."

"What I can't imagine," Bobby said, eyes forward, "is how I can get the hots for the husband of a woman I admire, who is, in any case, far too old for me. The husband, I mean, not the woman. And if you come up with some Freudian thing about fathers, I'll never speak to you again. Except in the line of duty, of course."

"Bobby, why not tell me what the rest of the problem is? It's not just Reed, although you do have a crush on him."

"A CRUSH!"

"I withdraw that patronizing word. You feel drawn to him, you like to be with him, you want him, or think you do. It's thrown some kind of spanner into the works; you're worried beyond your feeling for Reed, which ought, I think, to be both painful and pleasurable, like pushing your tongue against a sore tooth."

"I'm worried, Kate. I think I'm some sort of monster. Well, not monster really, but, well, not normal."

"*Normal* is absolutely my least favorite word," Kate said. "It is a statistical and conventional approximation, no more. When my mother was young, it was not normal to have intellectual ambitions, if one was a girl. Later normal meant being a virgin till you got married, and then moving to the suburbs. Normal is what sells fashions and face creams and other consumer items. Now that we've made that clear, what the hell are you worrying about, Bobby? I think you're great, apart from eyeing my husband, of course."

"I always hated being a girl. Not because I wanted to be a boy, but because I've always hated all the things girls are supposed to like: clothes, fashion, makeup, cooking, hostessing, gardening, sewing, being 'with it' in any way. I can't think it matters, well, if things go together, or if your hair is frizzy or straight, or about eye shadow. I'm being incoherent, I know. But more and more I felt that way; sometimes I met girls who agreed with me, or, even better, liked me even if they didn't agree with me. But I've always had to pretend 'feminine' interests which I don't feel. That's one of the reasons why I want to be a corporate lawyer. I'll have to dress up, but it will be a costume, the way I would have to wear a uniform if I joined the army. One day I hope I'll be a good enough lawyer to act the way I want and wear what I want." Bobby sighed.

"Surely you must know," Kate said, "how many young women

there are, women your age, who feel the same. My God, they're even in detective novels these days."

"Only written by much older women who are usually married and living in decorated houses."

Kate laughed. "Well, you may be right about that. Nonetheless, you're an accepted sort of character; you're you. Why not just be happy with that; Reed thinks you're great and I think you're great, and infatuations, maybe even obsessions, pass in time."

"If I was gussied up, Reed, just for an example, might take me seriously."

"Why on earth," Kate said, trying to keep the irritation from her voice, "should you want a man to take you seriously when you're being false to yourself? You can't have it both ways, as I dare say you know. You want permission to be your sort of woman, and yet you want to be the other sort for a man. That's not only illogical, it wouldn't even work. I promise you, Reed would far prefer you, or any woman, as herself. That's one of his most endearing characteristics, of which he has many. Bobby, there has to be more to this than what you've said."

"When I was a kid, I thought, well, that means I'm a lesbian. That's how everybody describes lesbians, isn't it? And then I turned out not to be, to want men, but not to want them all the time, not to be anybody's permanent acquisition. Oh, shit, I'm not making any sense."

"You're not," Kate said with some firmness. "Your view of lesbians, just for starters, is ridiculously stereotypical. Most of the lesbians I know adore cooking and flowers and dress like something out of *Vogue*. If the problem is deeper than you're managing to convey, maybe you need some sort of professional help, some sort of therapy. But I think you're just muddled, because of Reed and maybe other reasons I don't know about."

"You're right," Bobby said, sniffing. "I'm sorry."

"Now"—Kate assumed as chipper a manner as she could—"tell me what to expect when I get there. Not the woman, but what happens, what sort of a room do we meet her in?"

"Just an ordinary room; you sit across a table. You can't hand her anything but legal papers, nor she you, not even a letter to mail. That's a criminal offense. But there's no reason for you to hand each other anything."

"Can I take notes?"

"Yes. The only other thing, but Reed will tell you this, is do nothing without telling the client. I mean, Reed is the lawyer, and he has to keep his client up to date on everything. This is all rather confusing, since she's not his client yet."

"She seems to have studied literature in graduate school," Kate said, "so she's probably nutty as a fruitcake, like everyone who studies literature. If she had actually gotten a Ph.D., I would have given the case up as hopeless before we even got there. Oh, my, so this is what a prison facility is like?"

As they pulled up at the entrance and Bobby stopped the car to speak to the gatekeeper, she put out a hand and touched Kate. "Thank you," she said.

"Don't thank me," Kate said. "If you lay a hand on him, I'll kill you, of course; I'm a very jealous woman."

"You are a bit, aren't you?"

"Yes," Kate said. "But I try to deny it with every fiber of my being. What a horribly depressing place this is."

It seemed no less depressing as Kate sat facing Betty Osborne across a table in an otherwise bare and crumbling room.

"I don't suppose you have a cigarette," Betty said.

"I do, as a matter of fact." Kate handed over a pack of cigarettes. Reed had told her long ago that lawyers, even those who never smoked, always took cigarettes with them when interviewing prisoners in holding cells. They always wanted cigarettes, and had run out. She had remembered this, and lifted cigarettes from Harriet before setting out. Harriet had asked who they were for. Kate told her. "The best of all good luck," Harriet had said.

"Keep the pack," Kate now said to Betty Osborne.

"Only for now," Betty said. "I'm trying to give it up, I almost have, but I need to smoke under extreme stress; like this."

"You asked to see me. That needn't be stressful. Some people have even been known to talk to me without any stress whatever."

"I took one of your courses. A lecture, ten years ago maybe. I was getting my M.A. You talked about Hardy's women in a remarkable way. I remember that. Later you wrote a book on him, and I bought it and read it. I was taken with Hardy; you can see why." She laughed sharply. "I've become a Hardyesque heroine. Tess, that's me; we kill the men who do us wrong. Only they hung Tess, didn't they? I sometimes wish they could hang me."

"If you have turned into a self-pitying mess, there isn't much I can do for you, is there? It was not something Hardy's women allowed themselves."

Betty laughed again. It was a hollow laugh; Kate realized for the first time the condition that had inspired that cliché. Hollow, because there was no joy in it.

"Well," Betty said, "that's the script, I guess. You give me backbone, and persuade me to reopen my case. The thing is, I have a certain distrust of lawyers—hell, I detest them, them and doctors both—but I thought with you as a sort of intermediary, we might, well, at least talk about it. Not very invigorating, am I?"

"Didn't you plan to go on for your doctorate?"

"Sure, I planned to. I planned lots of things. And then I met this man—isn't that a cliché?—and we married, and I got pregnant, and then he started drinking, or started again, as I afterward learned, and beat up on me. Often, even when I was pregnant. And then in front of the kids. It's an old story by now, isn't it? Old and boring and hopeless."

"Where are the kids now?" Kate asked.

"With his parents. They got custody. They're not bad, it's probably the best arrangement. Of course, since I killed their son, I'm not exactly their favorite person. Probably you could guess that."

"Haven't you any family who could have helped out?"

"No. No one. This is home now. It's not as bad as it is for the women who have their babies in jail."

Kate found herself lost for words, an unfamiliar condition, but one that had occurred lately more than she might have expected. Perhaps we are likelier these days to face situations for which there are no words, she thought.

"Whatever the situation," she finally said, "I do think it would make sense to attack your conviction. I understand that you have a chance, under the now more general acceptance of the battered woman syndrome. Why not ask for Reed Amhearst as your lawyer, and give it a try?"

"Is that what you would do?"

"For God's sake," Kate exploded, "I haven't the least idea what I would do. I don't want to sound unsympathetic, and do please know that I'm not unsympathetic, but I have difficulty imagining staying with a man who battered me, even once. Which, of course, is a meaningless thing to say. I do understand how battered women become afraid, and victimized, and without any place or person to turn to. But since I'm not you, I don't know what I would do. Which is to say, if I were in your situation, I would certainly do everything I could to get my life back."

"I can't get my kids back."

"Even that isn't certain. If you are freed, the court would have to reconsider custody or at least visiting rights. Do you think you're free of him now—not literally free, of course you're that—but free inside yourself of dependence on such a man? I mean, Betty, if you were a character in a Hardy novel, you would have to ask yourself that, and answer yourself."

"And if I were a character in a Hardy novel, I would try to get my conviction thrown out?"

"I think so."

"It's more complicated than that."

"Tell me why."

Betty lit another cigarette and sat back, blowing the smoke ceilingward. "Have you read my case?"

"No," Kate said. "I haven't. I'm sorry. I was just told, a short time ago, that you wanted to see me, and that I had to come right away or permission for me to see you might be postponed. So here I am, sympathetic but uninformed."

"My husband taught at that law school, the same one that now has that clinic. Pretty funny, don't you think?"

"Very," Kate said. "Tell me about him."

"That's it, you see. I got a job there, at the law school, as his secretary. His secretary had to be smart, and flexible, and intelligent enough to know what was going on in his life. He was connected to a law firm as well as teaching, and needed someone to keep track of things. What he needed, of course, was a wife, as both of us figured out before long. He didn't bother mentioning, however, that he'd had a drinking problem. He'd been to AA, but he reverted under the strain of the new relationship. I think that's how they put it."

"Who put it?"

"His wonderful colleagues at Schuyler Law. Have you met any of them?"

"Yes," Kate said, "not a madly attractive bunch."

"I call them a scary bunch. I mean, nice as pie when you first meet them, but covering each other's asses, and their own, was the first order of business. And the last, of course. They testified that I drove him crazy, cheated on him—I didn't, but they manufactured evidence—and generally made the court believe that I not only got beaten by Fred out of a kind of sad desperation on his part, but that I was lying about him, and so on. I wouldn't let them put the kids on the stand, which I guess was noble but dumb. It was those law-professor colleagues of Fred's who did for me. That, and what the appeals court kept calling imminence, which means he wasn't beating me to death at the time I shot him. Of course not. I waited until the bastard passed out, and then I did it."

"Where did you get the gun?"

"From this guy I knew—well, I'd known him before. He was a graduate student, in political science. We met when we were students; he was a friend. I ran away once, and he was the only one I could think to go to. I knew where he had lived, and he was still there. He got me the gun. He said, 'Next time he goes for you, shoot him.' I never asked where he got the gun. They're not hard to get, are they?"

"No," Kate said, "they're not. And that was the guy you were supposed to be being unfaithful to Fred with?"

"They hired private detectives, those colleagues of his. They followed me. I used to go to see my friend with the kids—I hated to leave them alone or worse, with their father. They made that into something seamy. He was a friend, that's all. I should have had a woman friend, I guess. I had had them, but they all married and moved away. I was only at the graduate school for a year."

"Where did you grow up, come from?"

"Massachusetts. I left there a long time ago."

"What I'd like," Kate said, lighting one of the cigarettes and cursing herself, "is to persuade you to go ahead with a habeas corpus, a term I've only just got my mind around. Talk to Reed and his students, however it works, maybe only one of his students, maybe only Reed, I don't honestly know, but do it, go with it, take a chance."

"I don't need custody of the kids," Betty said, as though she were only catching up with the conversation on some sort of replay. "They're in school; they'll both probably be in college by the time I get out of here, if I ever do. It would be up to them if they wanted to see me. I keep remembering them as younger. As they were. I'd just have my own life to go on with. Suppose I wanted to go back for a Ph.D. Would you help me?"

"Yes," Kate said. "That's the first question you've asked me that I can answer with any assurance of knowing what I'm talking about. And, I think if you express a desire for the clinic's help, you can have it. Notice I said 'I think.' But there's a good chance. Think about it."

"I will. I'll think about it. Could you send me another copy of your book on Hardy?"

"Of course," Kate said. "But what about Hardy himself? Shall I send you some of his novels?"

"No. I can't bear reading novels, not good novels. I like reading literary criticism, but of course there isn't any around here."

"I'll send you a selection. That's too bad, about not reading novels, I mean."

"They're too powerful. They make me feel too hopeless. And I don't like the escape ones, which a few of the women here read. But literary criticism is, well, like a veil I watch literature through. I don't want to read about anyone killing anyone, or even hating anyone. Or loving anyone. Peculiar, I guess."

"Not really. Do you watch television? Do they let you?"

"We can, at certain hours. But I don't like that either. I try to keep my brain from going soft."

"And there is no one to send you any books?"

"My friend sends them, once in a while. But I haven't known what to ask him for. You've reminded me."

"I'll see that you get the books," Kate said, "and I'll be in touch. Or, if they don't allow me to come back, I'll send you messages through the clinic or write you letters by regular mail. I think that's allowed. And you write to me if you feel like it."

"Maybe I will. Thanks for coming. I think I asked for you because I thought you wouldn't come, but I'm glad you did. I think I'm glad. I'll let you know. You'll hear."

Driving back, they didn't talk much. Bobby kept her eyes on the road and the even heavier traffic. "I think she'll ask the clinic to take up her case," Kate said, when they were almost home. "I hope so. Perhaps you can see her soon, if you put her name on the list and get the coordinator's permission, and all the rest of it."

"We'll try," Bobby said.

They drove a bit longer in a silence punctuated only by the action of gears and brakes. Kate leaned back against the headrest and, as was her habit, let the day roll through her mind, like a film she could stop when something puzzled her.

"How did she know to ask for me?" Kate said suddenly, just as Bobby undertook a particularly tricky maneuver into another lane. "How did she know you knew me?"

"She heard Reed's name," Bobby finally said, when they had achieved the other lane, which immediately ground to a halt. "From some other prisoner, probably, or maybe she caught sight of him in the prison and asked who he was. As soon as she heard his name, yours, of course, followed like night the day."

"Why should it have?"

"Because as a student, I suppose, she was interested enough in you to find out all she could about you. Students often are that interested, you know. Finding out you were married and to whom hardly required rare detective talents."

"Reed seems to have been the key to today's conversations between us," Kate said. "I mean you and me. I hope all goes well with you, I really do."

"But sometimes," Kate muttered under her breath when they finally reached their destination, "I wish we'd never heard of the Schuyler Law School."

❦❦ 9

I invested my life in institutions—he thought without rancor—and all I am left with is myself.

—JOHN LE CARRÉ
SMILEY'S PEOPLE

Before the following week's class, Reed had been able to report to Kate that Betty Osborne was considering reopening her case. Blair and Kate approached the room with a sense of being ready for anything, except, as Blair pointed out, being locked in.

"On my insistence, they've removed the lock, I'm glad to say," Blair told her. "Enough is enough. After you," he added, holding the door for Kate with her briefcase.

It was fortunate that Kate and Blair had prepared themselves for the unexpected, because it soon became clear that the class had moved into a new phase and was ready to take on legal questions involving gender at full blast.

The class had read *Bradwell v. Illinois* for today, the Supreme Court's first case concerning a woman's claim to full participation in society, as Herma Hill Kay had put it. Kate had been very taken with Herma Hill Kay, who had written the casebook on sex-based discrimination and who was now dean of Stanford's law school. Myra Bradwell had applied for a license to practice law, which the Illinois Supreme Court had denied her because she was female. Bradwell was a lawyer, and her husband, who supported her law career, wished her to join him in his law practice. Justice Miller

wrote the opinion denying her this, on the grounds that "The para-
mount destiny and mission of woman are to fulfill the noble and
benign offices of wife and mother. This is the law of the Creator."
Herma Hill Kay had won Kate's admiration by wryly commenting,
in her casebook: "Although the method of communication between
the Creator and the judge is never disclosed, 'divine ordinance' had
been a dominant theme" in justifying sex-based discrimination.

The class today was to discuss the role of religion in legal discrimination against women in Bradwell, several cases previously
read, and *Jane Eyre*. As it turned out, Kate had spent longer on *Tess
of the d'Ubervilles* with Betty Osborne than this class would spend
on *Jane Eyre*. The class wanted to discuss the Schuyler Law School,
and the rights of women and minority students therein.

"All right," Blair said, pushing his books and papers aside. "If a
class can't discuss real life once in a while, it's not a class, it's a
habit," he said. Kate wrote for a moment on a piece of paper and
slid it across the desk toward him. It said: *There may be other tape
recorders running.* Blair contemplated the note for a minute, scrib-
bled on it, and passed it back while calling on the first student.
"Let's have a little order, however," he said. "One at a time, at
least at first."

His note read: *I've got tenure and you're out of here at the end of
the semester, so. . . .*

But order was hardly to be maintained. The students had se-
lected a spokesperson, a young woman who had marshaled her
thoughts and was ready; but it was clear, from the palpable energy
emanating from the group who could hardly sit still, let alone remain silent, that feeling was running high.

They did let her begin. "No woman has ever been chosen as *Law
Review* editor," she said. "You might not believe it, but we never
noticed that until you came, Kate. They always said it was the guy
with the highest grades, but last year there was a woman who was
sure she had the highest grades; we thought she was just a pain in
the ass, but now we wonder."

Kate, like the rest of the class, looked questioningly at Blair. She knew from Reed that the editor of *Law Review* used always to be the student with the highest grades, but that not terribly intelligent (in Kate's view) criterion had given way to someone with high grades and something else—energy, originality, daring, interesting origins. Schuyler Law, it seemed, was not only following the old custom, but cheating at it.

Nor was that all. The women students had begun exchanging stories of faculty moves on them, each woman considering herself alone in this until they had begun to talk to one another. "Women talking to one another are dangerous," Kate said when some comment was demanded of her. "That's why men liked to isolate us in separate houses and make us identify with the men rather than with each other. Women comparing notes frighten men. Auden said that somewhere. That's one of the reasons, though not the main one, women were supposed to be virgins at marriage: the men didn't want any basis for comparison."

"I also get the feeling," another woman student said, "that the faculty feels that since they had to let women in, if only to have enough students, they might as well get good use out of them." Blair grinned at Kate and pointed to her note. Kate shrugged her shoulders, returning the smile. Then everyone started speaking at once.

"Hold it," Blair shouted, standing up with his arms straight out, "hold it. I think we better go around the room, starting with you." He pointed to a young woman in the back and at the center of the table. "Then we'll move around to the left. You each have one minute to speak, so collect your thoughts. A minute is longer than you might imagine. Abigail?"

Abigail was a self-contained young woman who had struck Kate as competent and likely to do whatever would serve her own ends best. Not that Kate usually read character across a room, but it was a type she had known all her life. They went along with convention, and convention these days meant you could become a lawyer, but you would still be married in white, have a child in the first few years of marriage, and give it the husband's name. Any questioning of these items would be damned as useless, silly struggles. Abigail was not a woman who dealt in symbols.

"I'm not a feminist," she began, confirming Kate's guess. "But since we women pay as much as the men here, I think we should be treated equally, and not as though they were doing us a favor letting us in. That is how we feel, because of the way we are treated in class, because we are never spoken to seriously by the faculty, because we are never elected to any committees or posts. Some of the men students might elect us—not many, but some—but the faculty discourage them from supporting women. We've established that." Having said this, she stopped. She might not be inclined to stick her neck out, but she knew her rights and wanted them, as Kate had surmised.

Next to her was a young man who had been clearly unhappy in the class and, while not as outraged as Jake the door locker, was obviously fed up. He had so far contained himself, Blair later explained to Kate, because he, Blair, was his chief faculty adviser and able to help him in many ways. But by now he had clearly had enough of Kate.

"What makes you think you know any more about literature than we do?" he asked her, pointedly and rudely. Blair started to object to the tone if not the question, but Kate stopped him.

"What makes you think you, or Blair, know more about law than I do?" Kate asked.

"We've studied law," he said. "Anyone can read. As it happens, I've read a lot."

"Have you read *Jane Eyre* for today?" Kate asked.

"Sure," he said, although he knew, and he knew Kate knew, he had read it, if at all, sometime in the past.

"Why, then," Kate asked, "do you think the book ends with the word *Jesus*?"

He shrugged. "They all believed in religion in those days. They paid it lip service."

"Perhaps you're right," Kate said. "But how then do you account for Jane's answer to Mr. Brocklehurst when he warns her that if she is bad she will go to hell when she dies?"

"I don't account for it, I just listen to you blab on about it."

"Exactly," Kate said. "We both read, we both read and study texts. Yours are law texts, mine are literature. It's possible to read literature attentively and intelligently without studying it, and as I understand it, people used to be able to become lawyers by reading law while practicing it in a lawyer's office, no schooling needed. Isn't it just that we can't all do everything, so we learn from one another?"

"That's shit," he said, still sitting in place, looking, Kate thought, as though he might quite literally go up in smoke.

"Please feel free to leave, Ted," Blair said. "But just go; don't stop to try to beat me up, and don't try to lock the door behind you. Do not pass go; do not collect two hundred dollars."

It was unclear whether Ted was going to follow these orders, or sit and stew. To everyone's relief, however, he gathered up his books and stomped out.

"Next?" Blair sweetly said.

Somehow that outburst had helped the class to reveal what was on their minds; and, having spent their anger vicariously, they could talk calmly. Their complaints were all on the same theme, with variations. There ought to have been a woman faculty member appointed to replace Nellie Rosenbusch. Problems particular to women ought to be discussed. Rape and marital problems ought not to be the stuff of male humor in class. Faculty members should not flirt with women students, let alone come on to them.

Here there was an objection voiced. "Plenty of women law students have married their professors," a young woman near Kate remarked. "My friends tell me there are examples in every law-school faculty, men, that is, whose wives were their students. I don't think we ought to get too sweeping about this." The students all looked to Kate for her answer.

"Relationships are one thing," Kate said. "Sexual harassment is another. I can't really believe any of you wouldn't be able to tell the difference. But at least in literature departments where I have been, there are graduate students who want to marry professors who are already married; sometimes, often, these professors leave their wives and marry the student. The student often learns soon enough, having become the wife, that some other graduate student will try to displace her. Perhaps that doesn't happen anymore, however," she added. "I'm sometimes not quite up to date about current mores."

"Well," the young woman said, "I think we make too many laws about everything."

"I think so, too, sometimes," Kate said. "But in attempting to make the laws against harming certain people, we do inform ourselves about the possibilities of such harm. So the debate serves its purpose, although I end up on your side."

The young woman, to Kate's pleasure, smiled her agreement. God, Kate thought, how much we want them to appreciate us, to admit, however silently, to having learned something.

Eventually, they got around to a young man who would be almost the last person to speak. Kate metaphorically held her breath; she liked him, and hoped he would not go the way of the other two outraged young men, though if he did so, he would go politely.

"I'm interested in the question you asked Ted," he said. "About *Jane Eyre*. Why is the last word in the book the name of Jesus? Jane hated the hypocrisy of religion, and when she needed divine guidance, it was a woman god, the moon, who spoke to her. So why end with Jesus?"

"Do you have an explanation?" Kate asked.

"Well, I think it was a cop-out. She was scared she was writing too revolutionary a book, so she dragged Jesus in at the end. I don't exactly blame her, considering it was 1847, but I'm sorry she did it."

"You could well be right," Kate said. "I haven't an answer that I'm satisfied with for more than a week at a time. But that last paragraph does begin with a reference to St. John, whom Jane refused to join in a celibate marriage. She gave up religion for a relationship that allowed her her sexuality. But perhaps, having now got the sexuality, she was ready to reconsider religion?"

The young man laughed. "I still think it was a cop-out," he said.

"Okay," Kate said. "I still think you may be right."

On her way upstairs to Blair's office and her belongings—he had stayed behind to consult with a student—Kate was waylaid by Harriet. "How did it go at the prison?" she asked.

"Better than I might have hoped," Kate said. "She was grateful for the cigarettes. She might even decide to open her case with Reed's help. Why do you ask?"

"I'm interested in everything, like Walt Whitman," Harriet said. "Actually, I stopped you to say that I think we ought to have a meeting."

"We are having a meeting. Do you prefer to sit down, or retreat to the women's room as usual?"

"No, you clown, a meeting of all of us—you, me, Reed, Blair, and Reed's assistant at the clinic. Just to make sure we're all together on this, that we all know what's going on."

Kate looked surprised, or perhaps dubious.

"What I really want is some more of that malt scotch," Harriet said, "and this seemed like a good way to get it. Humor me. Ask us all for a drink today."

"All right," Kate said, "I'll try. I'll call Reed first and ask about him and Bobby, then I'll ask Blair, and then, if all goes well, I'll swoop you up and take you home and force single-malt scotch down your throat."

"You are an admirable woman, I've always said so," Harriet announced. "I await your swoop."

Reed was, as it happened, agreeable to meet them at home for a drink, and he promised to bring Bobby. Blair was always ready for a social occasion—so Kate had discovered—and swooping up Harriet having already been arranged for, they all arrived at the apartment at about the same time. Kate went for the single-malt scotch, which everyone except Bobby, who didn't drink, had agreed on—Kate actually, to her delight and surprise, managed to dig up a bottle of ginger ale for Bobby—and they all settled down to exchange stories.

"I take it Kate has told you about our fisticuffs and verbal onslaughts," Blair said to Reed. "Any idea that Schuyler Law might be a dull place has been banished, largely thanks to Kate, I do believe."

"It can't be due to me," Kate said. "I've lived a life amazingly devoid of physical exertion, if you don't count walking. People don't actually hit people in English departments, not at least in my presence. They take out their aggressions in squash games with their friends, and they simply ignore their enemies, or mouth sweet insincere nothings if they have to talk to them."

"And which group are you in?" Harriet asked, with a certain edge to the query.

"Oh, me for the meaningless sweet nothings," Kate said, unperturbed. "You'd be surprised all the same at how long it took me to figure out that promises meant nothing. But I was always allowed to do my own thing, so to speak. I mean, nobody intruded into the classroom or told me what I had to teach, or how I ought to teach it."

"I know what it's like," Reed surprisingly said. "That's why I left the DA's office. I started there soon after law school, when Hogan was still district attorney. He knew how to run the office. His assistant district attorneys were trained, they were supervised, their court appearances were watched and discussed afterward, it was a tight ship. Hogan quit as DA in 1973—he died in 1974—and I stayed on for a while. I tried to act as we all did under his leadership, but the place had gone sloppy, it became a stepping-stone for ambitious young politicos. It took a while to fall apart, but the young attorneys just counted on the police evidence, they didn't really prepare their cases, they didn't even always follow changes in the law. It got to be depressing. We had evolved from automatically hiring white males to hiring minority men and women both white and black, but there wasn't any discipline anymore, no real caring for the job. It took me a while to catch on to the fact that things were getting a lot worse, not better, and then I left. I went on to the academic world, which I have to admit is a much less demanding job, even if you do it properly. Or, I should say, it was less demanding, until this particular adventure came along. Oddly enough, the law professors at Schuyler Law remind me of the new crew in the district attorney's office: nothing matters but what we can say on our résumés, the contacts we make, and covering our asses."

Kate stared at him. "I never knew you felt that way," she said. What the words meant, as he well knew, was: you never told me that was how you felt, and now you're telling me in a group.

Reed answered the unasked question. "The odd thing is, I never really thought of my experience there in quite that way. I thought I was getting too old for the job, which I was, and getting cranky, which I was, and after Kate and I had been married awhile, I just left. But I didn't face what it was really about until just now. Hence the uncharacteristic speech." He looked at Kate as though to say: "Sorry." She nodded consolingly.

"It's like long marriages," Harriet added, "where the woman suddenly walks out, to everyone's astonishment, including her own. She's never allowed herself to recognize what was going on, or that she'd outgrown the whole arrangement, or that she was now a quite different person. And when she does realize it and walks away, she looks back on the long years of marriage and interprets them quite differently. As you did with the DA," she added to Reed.

"If we're going to discuss marriage, I was lured here under false pretenses," Blair said, "and so, I can see by the way she sips her ginger ale, was Bobby. The scotch is excellent, but I'm a bit nervous about the agenda."

"No, you're not, you just want to talk about beating up students in your class. Fine behavior, I must say." Harriet looked hopefully at the bottle, and Reed, smiling, filled her glass.

"There's no doubt, my dears, the faculty are worried about a new ripple of discontent in the student body, all of it attributed to Kate and Reed, but really to Blair, who got them there. If," she added, looking at Blair, "I had a nickel for every time they regretted hiring you with tenure, I'd have a ride on the subway, maybe both ways."

"What is it exactly that we're supposed to have done?" Blair asked.

"Well," Harriet said, "teaching, or as they think of it, indoctrinating the students with feminist cases and feminist lit crit, just for starters. Then there's all this locked-door business. Naturally, they take no responsibility for the student who locked the door and grappled with Blair, and I think they have more than a suspicion that whatever Reed is doing out at the prison for women is not going to be conducive to their peace of mind. Of course, this is all interpolation and translation. Most of what I hear is grunts and groans, with an occasional expletive, but the infrequent word serves to clarify the message."

"All that is normal faculty justification," Blair said. "As to Reed's clinic, they think it's a waste of time to teach law students what they can learn on their own when they get out."

"And," Harriet said, "they are worried about that poor battered woman incarcerated on Staten Island who was married to one of their group and who they fervently hope—I'm surmising this—will not talk to Reed or anyone in his clinic."

"As it happens," Reed said, "Betty Osborne has asked to see Kate again. I'm sorry I haven't had a chance to mention it to you before," he said to Kate. "Things seem to be moving rather fast all of a sudden."

"I've noticed," Kate said, trying to keep any edge from her voice.

"One other thing they've taken to objecting to," Blair said into the silence, "is the number of aging students who are flocking to the law school."

"Women who have returned to law school after an unhappy life as a housewife," Harriet said. "I've noticed them, and I must say I cheer them on when I can."

"Actually," Blair said, "the script goes this way: she's put him through graduate school, provided him with invaluable professional help, and raised the children; now he's decided she isn't suited to his new, more glamorous and successful life. So he marries someone twenty or thirty years younger than he is, and the abandoned wife is totally miserable for a year or two, and then one day she discovers that it was the best thing that ever happened to her, especially if she has managed to get some income out of the divorce and if the children are on the way to independence."

"You seem well-informed on the subject," Harriet said.

"I am," Blair said. "It happened to my mother. I followed her into the law, as it happens. I was one of the children more or less on the way to independence. She didn't seem to think much of the way the law and the courts regarded women, and I rather ended up agreeing with her."

Kate looked at him with renewed interest. She knew that neither she nor Reed had spoken as much as was their wont. She felt, and was fairly certain that Reed felt also, that they had to talk with one another as soon as they could. She found herself wishing the others would go, but recognized the unreasonableness of this; she had agreed to this meeting and would have to see it through.

But, Kate was moved to notice, Harriet had picked up Kate's wishes, and began to gather her wits and her belongings in an obvious way. "Great," she said, draining her glass and rising determinedly to her feet. "Let's all get to it. Blair and Kate will continue their wonderful seminar, without physical activity if possible, if not, with. You two," she said to Reed and Bobby, "figure out your Betty Osborne strategy before too long, hear? I'm glad to have met you, Bobby. Why don't the three of us wander off together to a comfortable bar and tell each other our lives and miracles?" And gathering up the others with a glance, like an English upper-class hostess ready at the end of a formal dinner to depart with the women, she marched them to the door. The good-byes were brief.

Kate and Reed sank back side by side on the couch after Reed had poured them each another drink.

"Sorry about that," he said, taking her hand. "About the confessions regarding the DA's office and the rest of it. I hope you understand that its suddenly coming out that way was as much of a surprise to me as to you. I hope believing that reduces the jolt a little."

"It *was* a jolt," Kate said. "But I do begin to see that, like most women, I've blamed myself for something that has as much to do with you as with me, and probably much more. We women, however modern, liberated, and deep into analysis of the patriarchy and all its workings, still seem to assume our own guilt and our own responsibility for healing in every damn situation that comes along."

"I don't blame you for being angry," Reed said. "You're right; I do see that."

"See what?" Kate said, her tone indicating doubt that he did see.

"See that in some crazy way, my willingness to take on the clinic at this damn law school was a way of forcing the whole mess out in the open. Does that make any sense? Perhaps we should take a vacation together, if this mess is ever resolved, and just talk."

"I don't believe in vacations," Kate said. "I don't even like them. And if two people are living together and, in theory at least, are devoted to each other, if they can't talk about what's eating them during the course of everyday life, they probably never will. The point is, I suppose, that vacations offer time for conversation, but as far as I'm concerned, what they mainly offer is excuses to avoid conversation, or a way to feel a little less bored with your usual companion, changing the setting to stimulate interest, which it doesn't."

"The hell with vacations, then," Reed said.

It was, after all, Reed who, the next day, drove Kate to the Staten Island prison to confer (for *absolutely* the last time, he promised) with Betty Osborne. They decided to take the ferry; it certainly wasn't quicker, but it seemed to fit their mood better than the Verrazano Bridge; standing at a rail, looking at water, always reminded Kate of the old movies they had taken to renting and watching into the night. Lovers stood at the rails of ships, in the days when that was how people traveled, and waxed romantic. It wasn't reality; nothing could have been further from reality, but at least one could watch those movies without inevitably retiring to nightmares. Kate also found black-and-white films restful, to say nothing of the fact that, unlike life and current movies, one scene plainly ended before another began.

So once on the ferry they left the car and climbed the stairs to the highest deck. New York and the Statue of Liberty were spread around them. Kate admitted to herself that it reminded her more of the immigrants' journey to Ellis Island than an erotic interlude on an Atlantic steamer, but she felt happy nonetheless. (Later, when she mentioned the ferry ride to Harriet, Harriet recalled Smiley's words on the matter: it was a habit of the spying trade, Smiley had decided; spies talk better when there's a view.) But Kate and Reed were not talking of the spying trade.

"Let me give it one more try," Reed said, "explaining to myself and you what happened to me. It's not the usual midlife crisis, I'm sure of that. It isn't a man saying to himself, 'Is this all there is?' It isn't the depression of some scientists I know who wake up to the fact that if they haven't had a Nobel Prize by this age, they never will. You have to understand, Kate, that I wasn't aware I was unhappy; I think I just began to fade away, to become less distinct, without really noticing it, even though fading away was making me miserable."

"You never seemed to me in the least danger of fading away," Kate said.

"No. The outer man remained the same. Here's what I think it was. I don't understand it all yet, but I think I have a clue. I was becoming comfortable in the status quo, one of the boys, one of the establishment, no threat of danger. Well, *danger* is too strong a word. I had become one of the regular guys, part of a self-satisfied, largely mediocre clump cemented together by the ease and superficial congeniality of our life. It wasn't that way at the DA's; we kept lurching from one case to another, we had to be on our toes, indolence alternated with amazing effort. There was no time, for the most devoted of us anyway, to just go on doing what we were doing. And, of course, we weren't paid handsomely; we hadn't made it."

"I know," Kate said. "I've felt all that."

"Not in the same way, don't you see?" Reed said, putting his arm around her. "You always had the challenge of being a woman, of being a feminist, of trying to change the system, trying to open it up. You aren't the kind of woman who felt easy just being one of the boys."

"I doubt any woman feels easy with that," Kate said. "Not really."

They were quiet for a minute, and then, taking her completely by surprise, Reed kissed her. Not lightly, but as though they were on an Atlantic steamer, in love but threatened with separation. I'd forgotten about kisses, Kate thought, astonished and amused at her response. I'd forgotten what they were like before movies forever hooked the erotic to the explicitly sexual. By god, I'd forgotten.

The ferry horn blasted; they were docking.

"Shall we let them push the damn car into the sea?" Reed asked. But they had already started down the stairs, laughing together.

Betty Osborne seemed glad enough to see Kate, but she sat silently, reminding Kate of how her mother used long ago to say, "Cat got your tongue?" when the recalcitrant child Kate refused to discuss the matter at hand. Betty was not recalcitrant, only at a loss for words, and Kate did not know how to help. She had already made the general inquiries that were supposed to begin the conversation, but seemed, instead, to have shut it down.

Since they had limited time, Kate decided that after all, she had better prime the pump. "If you don't know where to begin," she said, "why not start with what you remember of the law school where your husband taught? Did you know his colleagues well?"

"Some of them," Betty answered. "But I've been thinking about Tess. Do you suppose I'm crazy at a time like this to be thinking about a character in a novel a hundred years old? I could have got the book to read, as you suggested, but I only wanted to remember it."

"If I thought you were crazy to think of Tess, I would have to think my whole life was crazy and worthless into the bargain," Kate said, "and I don't. What was it you felt about Tess?" Betty had talked of Hardy at her previous visit, Kate remembered.

"What I thought is all mixed up with what critics said. We read so many critics in graduate school, and some of them seemed to say exactly what I had thought. I remember you told us we had to footnote the book anyway, even if we'd thought of what the book said before we read it."

Kate smiled her interest. Betty had begun talking and might continue. After a pause, she went on, almost as though Kate were not there.

"Remember that Hardy had subtitled the novel 'A Pure Woman,' and later regretted it? Of course you remember. I think the trouble is that Tess and I, we were pure women, really, and not prepared for the world we had to face. Tess's honesty cost her everything, and in the end she, too, murdered the bastard. They hung her; they don't hang people anymore, so the way I figure it is, maybe that means that I have another chance."

She looked at Kate to see if she agreed. Kate nodded.

"One critic," Betty continued, "one I remember particularly, compared Tess's journey to *Pilgrim's Progress*. Probably many critics said that. And that same critic pointed out that Tess's pilgrimage had no goal, no way of ending satisfactorily. That was Tess's tragedy, and I guess it was mine. Neither Tess nor I seemed to fit into any of the usual categories for women; that's probably why Hardy didn't like his subtitle. She wasn't pure or impure, she wasn't anything a woman was supposed to be. Except a victim. That's what Tess was, that's what I was, a victim. But she only seems to be a victim—you told us that—because she does something about her life. She refuses just to be passive."

She looked up at Kate, who again nodded, smiling encouragement.

"I mean," Betty went on, "it's all there. The birds left to die, with no one caring, killed for the fun of it; the poor animals in the hay field after it's mowed, trapped and clubbed to death. The rats—were they rats?—in the corn rick. And Tess most of all, laid out like a sacrifice at Stonehenge. Maybe you were wrong and Tess was a victim because she never thought about escaping, not ever, not even at the end. So what I thought"—here, Betty paused and looked up at Kate—"what I thought is maybe I should think of ways to escape. Maybe I don't have to be a victim like the animals in the hay field, like the birds, like Tess at Stonehenge."

Bless you Thomas Hardy, Kate thought with reverence. One thing I have that Reed doesn't is the very occasional assurance that literature matters. Reed always knows the law matters, so it becomes incapable of suddenly revealing its significance.

"Reed thinks there's a good chance the case can be reopened," Kate said. "He's going to do his best, and you should, too. If the hundred years between you and Tess haven't got us the right to appeal, well, that would be too bad, wouldn't it?" Kate, quite against prison rules, held out a handkerchief to Betty, who took it, crying freely now.

"You're right," Betty said into the handkerchief. "I've decided. There's no point in just giving up; I've got to try. At the end, Angel says to the police, let her finish her sleep. Well, I'm not going to finish my sleep. That is, if you think that's the right move."

"Of course it is," Kate said, trying to sound matter-of-fact. "You have to talk it all over with Reed; he has to decide how to go about it. But I'm hopeful, I really am."

"They all lied," Betty said. "All of Fred's friends at the school. They said he never beat me, that I was crazy, and made scenes, and drank, and neglected the children. They all testified, lying through their teeth. Do you think Reed can do anything with that?"

"Perhaps we can find some witnesses the defense should have called and didn't," Kate said. "But I'm not a lawyer, and law isn't justice. Still, it sounds promising."

"There were people at the school who knew what Fred was like.

But they were afraid to say anything; they were mostly secretaries. Do you think they might help now; do you think they might remember?"

"I can't pretend to know, Betty, but I certainly think they might be willing to. I don't know much of anything about the law, but if Reed is hopeful that you have a chance, then you do have a chance, and he'll know what to base it on. I'm very glad you asked to see me. I hope the next time I see you, it will be away from here, somewhere you have chosen, somewhere nice." Kate had glanced at her watch, and knew her time was almost up. Reed still had to talk to Betty.

"Be sure to tell Reed all you've told me—about the case, I mean —and everything else about it you can think of," Kate said. "He's the one who matters when it comes to getting them to allow an appeal."

"I know," Betty said. "But I wanted to talk to you about Tess. I didn't think he'd know about her, and I knew you would. It must seem stupid, thinking about a novel that way. It's almost as though I knew her, watching her life destroy itself."

"I'd rather have talked to you about Tess," Kate said, "than read a hundred critical essays on Hardy."

"But I think the essays helped me to understand the book, helped me to remember what was important about it." Betty might be ready to attack law professors, but she meant to defend literary critics.

"I'm glad," Kate said, letting it go at that. "Don't go to sleep like Tess," she finally added. "Wake up."

"I have," Betty said, smiling, sad, but still smiling. "I've woken up."

Kate waited in the car for Reed while he talked to Betty. When he finally emerged, Kate closed her book and looked up at him inquiringly.

"You shook her up," Reed said. "I think we've got a chance for a retrial."

"I didn't shake her up," Kate said. "Thomas Hardy did."

"She never mentioned Hardy to me," Reed said. "Isn't Hardy one of the major authors you've written about?"

"You know what Betty Osborne is?" Kate said. "She's a pure woman, that's what she is."

"If you say so," Reed agreed. "I'm going to do my best to prove it. You drive, if you don't mind. I want to make some notes."

This time they went back by the bridge, eager to reach home.

🦚🦚 10

He knew of course. All of them had tacitly shared the
unexpressed half-knowledge which like an illness they hoped
would go away if it was never owned to, diagnosed.

—JOHN LE CARRÉ
TINKER, TAILOR, SOLDIER, SPY

As the semester progressed, landing them all eventually in sight of the end, three important announcements were made by the dean of Schuyler Law. They were made quietly, in a Xeroxed notice to the faculty that it was hoped would look innocuous, and perhaps remain unread not only by the faculty to whom it was directed, but by the student community as well. Blair gleefully announced to Kate—after, as he elegantly and originally put it, the shit had hit the fan—that the dean and those members of the faculty who comprised his main support did not yet realize that they had lost their control of Schuyler Law. The students were no longer going to do as they were told, and what had started as a fuzzy memo threatened to erupt into wide, highly regrettable publicity.

The announcements were, in substance: (1) that Professors Reed Amhearst and Kate Fansler would not be returning to Schuyler Law after this semester (this was hardly a surprise to anyone, since both had made it clear that they had come for one semester only and had not the smallest intention of returning); (2) that neither the new clinic dealing with the legal problems of prisoners nor the new course in law and literature would be continued after the pres-

ent semester; (3)—(the one that caused the most reaction by far)—
that a yearly prize, generously offered to Schuyler Law for the best
Law Review essay on the topic of law and gender, would be refused.

Blair, as a faculty member, received the memo and generously
distributed copies of it made for him by Harriet, who did not take
any measures to keep the memo out of the hands of students. The
result was an uproar such as Schuyler Law had never anticipated,
let alone experienced: the students called meetings and made post-
ers, replaced as fast as they were torn down, and increasing in
bluntness as resistance to them made itself evident.

The dean and his faculty comrades had not included among their
announcements the likely reconsideration of Betty Osborne's case,
but the thought of that, added to the publicity stew, improved neither their tempers nor, as became increasingly clear, their judg-
ment.

The prize they had turned down was an offering from Charles
Rosenbusch, Nellie's brother. He was the inheritor of Nellie's es-
tate, which included a life-insurance policy, taken out before her
illness had manifested itself. He determined to establish a prize in
her honor at the school in which she had struggled and, to some
degree, won. Before offering it to the school, he had discussed it at
some length on the telephone with Blair and then with Kate, both
of whom had helped to focus the wording of the prize. Income
from the capital would constitute the prize: a sum not negligible to
Schuyler's students. As an added insult, he had left the investment
of the capital to Blair rather than to the dean of the school, which
meant in effect that the dean had to agree to whatever investment
was decided upon for the money. Neither Blair nor Kate allowed
the students to have the least doubt as to the smallest detail about
the prize the dean had so cavalierly refused.

Needless to say, Kate and Reed, Harriet and Blair were, during
all the student uproar and the publicity that followed, pleased but
silent, letting the students carry the ball. ("Why is it," Kate asked
Blair, "that sooner or later we all resort to sports metaphors, even
if we haven't a clue as to what they mean in the game—in this case,

football?" Blair had pointed out that she certainly knew what it meant to carry the ball. "But I don't know how the carrier got the ball," Kate answered, always ready for a debate. "You do in this case," Blair answered. "That's why sports metaphors are so useful. We may not know squat about the sport, but we know what it means to get on the scoreboard." Kate decided not to pursue the subject further.)

The dean and the faculty decided to have a meeting of the entire school. This happened infrequently—in fact, only at graduation—for which purpose they were in the habit of repairing to a rented hall nearby. The meeting was called, and Reed and Kate, still faculty members, however temporarily, decided to attend, as did Harriet and those on her staff who could be persuaded that it was their business, too. Certainly it was a student protest, but the staff might one day want student support for their own ends. (The dean had, in fact, already decided to dispense with Harriet's services, efficient as she was, but had bided his time in telling her so; not that she needed telling, being a confidante of the dean's secretary and planning in any case to hand in her resignation at the semester's end.)

Above all, the dean strove, as the meeting got under way, for calmness. "Let us not interrupt one another," he said, "let us speak one at a time, above all let us remember what this law school means to us all."

The whole assembly listened to the defense of his actions in silence, a silence he should have found ominous but probably did not. When he had finished, a man stood up, announced himself as representing the students, and asked to deliver a statement no longer than the dean's and covering the same points. It was astonishingly clear that the dean had not expected this, and could think, in the light of his opening remarks, of no way to stop this evident disaster. Harriet commented to Reed, on her right, on the dean's stupidity, but Reed pointed out that when you have been in absolute power, you lose all sense that anyone can successfully contradict you.

"I shall take the dean's announcements as delivered to the faculty one by one," the student representative began. Blair whispered to Kate, on his left, that his name was O'Hara, and that he hoped to go to work for the DA.

"Don't tell Reed," Kate whispered back.

"I actually think," Blair hissed, "that he'll end up a public defender. He's seen the light."

"First, we already knew that Professors Amhearst and Fansler, known to us as Reed and Kate, will not be returning. We are very sorry and hope they will come again someday." (Loud applause and some cheering. "Do you suppose Jake is here?" Kate asked Blair. "I doubt it," Blair said. "He's probably writing a letter to your chairman trying to get you fired." "That's just what he's likely to do," Kate said. "How clever of you to guess.")

"While we shall certainly miss Kate and Reed, the class and clinic that brought them to Schuyler shall, we are determined, continue. That is our response to the dean's second announcement. Professor Blair Whitson will still be here to do the law and literature seminar with someone else, for whom remuneration funds will, we are confident, be provided. Reed has assured us that should the clinic he established be continued, he would help us to find another director. ("Did you?" Kate asked Reed, on her left. "More or less," he said, "but a long time before this uproar. Frankly, I assumed they would keep the clinic on.")

"We come now," the speaker continued, "to the prize offered for the best essay on law and gender, so strangely declined by the dean and the faculty. Why did they decline it? Because they do not consider gender a proper subject for an essay in the *Law Review*? Because they do not wish to discuss gender at all, preferring to have the fact that there are no tenured women on the faculty pass unnoticed? The dean gives no reason, and I am deeply puzzled to imagine what reason, apart from prejudice and a reluctance to change, he can have. I move that this body recommend to the dean the continuance of the clinic and the course on law and literature,

131

and the immediate acceptance of the prize offered by the late Nellie Rosenbusch's brother. All in favor say aye."

The rafters shook with all the *ayes* shouted. ("I never felt rafters shake before," Kate commented to Reed. "Me neither," said Blair, who overheard her. "Certainly not these rafters.")

"Such a motion is out of order," the dean shouted when the decibel count eventually lowered.

"It is not," said the student speaker. "I spent most of last night with *Robert's Rules of Order*."

"This is not a meeting in which such rules apply," the dean fairly screamed.

"Then I withdraw my motion temporarily, and replace it with a motion that this body agree to be in session for such a resolution. All in favor say . . ." Again the rafters shook with loud *ayes*. "We have to have a second before we vote; sorry about that," the student amended. "Do I have a second?" He had, the noise confirmed, a second. "Now, all in favor . . ."

Clearly the dean was shaking with the rafters. "I move that this meeting be adjourned," he screamed. "Seconded," shouted Professor Slade. The microphones were disconnected, the lights were turned off, all except for the exit signs, and the dean, together with most of the faculty, departed by way of the stage entrance.

"We better stay put if we don't want to be trampled to death," Harriet suggested. But, it soon became evident, they were less in danger of being trampled than engulfed. "What do we do now?" the students shouted at Kate and Reed and Blair. Blair, gathering from the glances of Kate and Reed that he had been appointed spokesperson, stood up.

"My advice," he said as the hall quieted down, "is to let the publicity do its work. My guess is that within a week you will have won all your points. If not, let's regroup. We've only got two more weeks to the semester and then exam period, so I suggest we take some action, if action is necessary, exactly one week from today. If you will elect a committee of three to represent you, I'll be glad to meet with you at that time."

After a certain amount of buzzing, this offer and advice were accepted. Kate and Reed and Harriet congratulated Blair. "I spoke to Charles Rosenbusch this morning," Blair told them, "and he promises that if his offer of the prize is refused, he'll make sure the press learns of it. Considering his dislike of publicity, that shows that he's determined on this matter. So, in case you hadn't gathered, am I."

When Kate and Reed finally made their way out of the hall and onto the street, they were happy to stroll together, feeling as though some hurdle had been passed, not just for Schuyler Law but for them, too.

"I heard something funny yesterday," Reed said. "They had an earthquake in Oregon awhile ago, not a profound one, but noticeable. And a friend, who'd come to town for a conference, said he and his wife, both hard workers who rarely reached home at the same time and who even less often had time to relax together, seated on their couch, had achieved this miracle on the day of the earthquake, and, he told me, 'As we were sitting side by side on the couch, the earth moved.' I rather liked it."

"You seem very chirpy," Kate observed. "Any other good news, apart from the earth moving in Oregon?"

"Yes. Thank you for asking. They've agreed to review Betty Osborne's case. I don't know what you said, Kate—she credited you completely for having reached the decision to try—but not only is she agreeing, she's come up with some lovely information making it quite clear that the defense did not use evidence they had, and the prosecution witnesses lied under oath. It's most promising."

"You think the jury will let her off this time?"

"No jury yet, my love. There will be a habeas corpus hearing, at which all the suppressed evidence will surface. We'll find out if the prosecution knew and deliberately suppressed it. After the hearing, a judge will probably vacate her conviction. A retrial is possible but not likely; if she wins on habeas, she could be retried. But I'm pretty sure the state won't retry her because, given the hanky-panky, the prosecution would be too embarrassed to try her again."

"What sort of suppressed evidence?"

"That people knew she had been battered, people at the school. That they brought pressure on her not to hire a different defense lawyer—they got to the one she had—and they took full advantage of the fact that she was in shock, having just shot her husband and lost her children. To say nothing of the fact that the battered woman syndrome was not evoked."

"Do you think she'll get the children back?"

"If she's exonerated she's got a good chance. Although the fact that she did shoot their father will always be a problem. That's not going to go away. But there is a best-possible outcome, and I hope we get it. Bobby has been very useful, by the way, and has worked hard on all fronts. I had a long consultation with her today, and we're both pretty certain that Betty Osborne will have another chance." -

"Will Schuyler Law survive in an improved state?"

"Oh, I think so," Reed said, "unless some other institution decides to take it over and is able to bring about some reforms."

"Well," Kate said, "I'm feeling after today's meeting that we accomplished more than we could have hoped. Maybe we became moles in the best le Carré tradition; certainly Schuyler never guessed what it was in for when they agreed to hire us. But I think we've made something moribund a little livelier."

"And getting the Osborne habeas through will always be something I'm glad I did," Reed said. "And I am convinced that clinic we started will make an important contribution to Schuyler, the students, and to some people in prison. Prisoners need good lawyers, the students learn a lot, and with Clarence Thomas on the Supreme Court, voting in favor of beating prisoners and letting them inhale smoke all day, we have to take some countermeasures, however few. The important thing is, I've got you back. I have, haven't I, Kate?"

"You never lost me, not really. I would have fought Bobby like a tiger for my man. Is she over that, you think, not that you ever admitted in so many words that she was in it in the first place?"

"Is any of us ever over anything? We get to the point where we can claim to be over things, and that's the best there is."

"Really," Kate said. "How circumspect you have become. I thought over was over."

"How's your over?" Reed asked. "What do you say to a ferry ride? We can climb up to the highest deck."

"Let's not and say we did," Kate responded, remembering a popular response from her childhood. Which shows, she thought, that even the most intellectual of devoted couples can become silly asses given the right motivation.

The next day, there was a message from Charles Rosenbusch, leaving his number. Kate called him back.

"I've never been so offended in my life," he said. "Not even when some famous critic insisted that Robert Frost was a better poet than Wallace Stevens."

"You don't like Frost?" Kate asked.

"Of course I like Frost, but it's perfectly idiotic to call him a better poet than Wallace Stevens. What on earth are we talking about? Do you have this effect on everybody?"

"I didn't say a word," Kate reminded him. "You can't blame me if you had to reach for a comparison to Schuyler's behavior."

"You're right, of course. I'm behaving badly. But by god, I'm going to make one hell of a fuss about this prize. They didn't kill Nellie, I told that truthfully enough, they didn't push her under the truck. But they certainly did their best to beat her down. I want you to advise me how to get the most publicity possible."

"After yesterday's meeting," Kate said—and she told him about it—"you may not have to do anything. I suspect that the school is going to have to back down on all its points, except not asking Reed and me back, and we hadn't the faintest intention of coming back anyway. Blair—you spoke to Blair—has arranged for a week to allow Schuyler gracefully to reverse itself, after which dreadful things are planned. Why don't you wait and see what happens in that week?"

"Sold," Rosie said. "Kate, I want to thank you. No, don't protest, I insist upon saying this. Your coming here, which must have seemed like a fool's errand when you did it, made a change for me. It shook me up. Not you or what you said, but just the fact of the intrusion, of speaking about Nellie, of realizing that I'd sunk into a mire of self-pity."

"I had nothing to do with all that," Kate assured him when he paused for breath. "I galloped off in all directions like an idiot, trying to prove a murder in the face of all the facts just because I needed to do something. If I inadvertently helped you, you helped me even more. In addition to which," she added in a concluding sort of voice, "I was presented with a book of poems inscribed by the author. I'm waiting eagerly for the next volume, which I hope you will also inscribe."

"You've got it," Rosie said.

11

*I didn't hear a sound beyond the confident flow of Smiley's
voice and the eager burst of laughter at some
unexpected self-irony or confession of failure. You're
only old once, I thought, as I listened with them,
sharing their excitement.*

—JOHN LE CARRÉ
THE SECRET PILGRIM

It was some days later that Kate summoned Harriet to a meeting
in her, Kate's, living room. Harriet, behaving like a perfect guest,
allowed the doorman to ring up and ask for admittance.

"I wondered when you'd decide to have it out," Harriet said.
Offered a drink, she declined firmly: her hour for imbibing was still
a long way off. "One has to have rules about these things," she said.

"I somehow got the impression you didn't believe in rules," Kate
remarked, offering coffee instead.

Harriet declined that also. "I've decided to ignore many rules of
our society, since, as far as that society knows, I've died and gone to
heaven. But I have my own system of morals and rules, every bit as
good and sometimes better."

Here she paused, in an attitude of attentiveness.

"Good news about Betty Osborne," Kate said, and told her what
Reed had reported.

"I'm really glad," Harriet said. "I worked a good bit with battered women, you know. It's horribly discouraging. I had to give it up."

"Why?"

"They all go back. They don't have anywhere else to go, they were probably beaten as children, or saw their mothers being beaten. No program I worked with, or any other, I bet, had the money to keep them more than thirty days at the most, and then they'd go back to the same old thing. They gave different reasons— he would reform, the children missed their father, it was home, and on through even sillier excuses, but the fact was they hadn't been given enough independence and enough training and counseling. Our wonderful society can't find the money to give it to them. After not very long, I got burned out, and I wasn't even doing it except as a volunteer."

"Are you saying that Betty Osborne hadn't a chance?"

"Not at all, my dear. Ms. Osborne shot the bastard. He isn't there to go back to, and anyway, she took charge of her own life, in a manner of speaking. Once she got into jail, I thought she would probably just rot there, punishing herself, but you see, you and Reed have made a difference. She's got a chance, one of the few."

They sat in silence for a moment.

"Tell me again why you came to New York," Kate said, breaking the silence.

"I told you that, dear Kate. Are you having memory lapses, and you so young and spry?"

"I know; the catalpa tree. Well, once in New York, what made you decide to sign on with Schuyler Law?"

"They offered to pay me well."

"With your organizational skills, any law firm would have been glad to hire you and pay you much better. Schuyler is hardly the most attractive ambience in the city."

"For one thing, I guessed that they wouldn't look too closely at my credentials; but the real reason was that I think clumps of medi- ocrity may be the sign of doom in our world, certainly in the academic world, and even more certainly in the world of law. I decided to have a go at it.

"I'll tell you how I see it," Harriet said, smiling at Kate. "They—mediocrities—decide to cling to a certain sense of what they are pleased to call principles. Always beware of people with principles. I don't mean general principles like the Golden Rule, or that Hebrew who stood on one foot and said something about treating one's neighbor as oneself. I mean people who grab on to a structure, usually one that's been in place, untested, for years, maybe for centuries, and feel so cozy inside it that they don't want to be moved out. That's why women have become so threatening, don't you see? If women move out, the whole structure has to be reorganized, and it might in turn lead to men being shoved out of their padded lives. My male academics decided to cling to some past system, whether of lit crit or patriarchy or Freud or law doesn't really matter, and to see any attempt to transform it as the beginning of the end. It certainly would be the end of them, the bastards, and they're smart enough to know it."

"So here you are in New York, fighting stupidity and evil at Schuyler Law," Kate said.

"I hope you aren't growing testy, Kate. It doesn't become you. I've always admired your cool. Anyway, as I frankly told you, I've taken a leaf from John le Carré and decided to act like George Smiley. I think, I brood, I organize. You know, the way he went after Karla in the end. I've taken Smiley as my model. I'm not as fat, probably taller, female, and with no intelligence service behind me, but I do my best with what I have. If Schuyler is really changed, as that meeting seemed to indicate it would be, I'll have performed my final act as part of the academic world. Smiley used many different names, and rented cars which got smashed up, and all sorts of other things I haven't been able to attempt. I've just done my best."

"And would you say that you've won, like Smiley?"

"I'd say we've all won. But Smiley knew, and I know, that no victory is final. Still, he got Karla and we got . . ."

"What did we get, Harriet? Do please say it."

"Really, Kate, you're not only having lapses of memory, you're repeating yourself. We all know what we've accomplished, we were all there at that wonderful meeting. Perhaps we both need a drink. The day is wearing on nicely, isn't it?"

"Let it wear on a bit longer."

"You're the hostess, you're the summoner," Harriet said, composing herself like patience on a monument.

"In all that time you were talking about the catalpa tree," Kate finally said, "and even today, talking about mediocrity, you never mentioned whether you and your husband had any children."

Harriet, abandoning her pose, stretched her legs out. "Ah," she said, "I wondered when you'd think of her."

"Her who?" Kate asked rather incoherently.

"Demeter, of course."

"Demeter." Kate, repeating the word, recognized that Harriet would always have the ability to spin her off balance.

"I thought you were familiar with Greek myths," Harriet said in a tone of disappointment. "Particularly that one. I thought you had it in mind all along. I really am disappointed in you, Kate."

They sat a moment in silence.

"It's not as though you ever mentioned Demeter," Kate said, light dawning.

"Well, hardly." Harriet sounded put out. "After all, I couldn't stop the crops from growing or make some other sort of bargain with the powers that be. Women haven't got that much leverage these days; I assumed you realized that."

"Yes," Kate said. "I think you had a right to assume I would remember Demeter. It's one of my favorite stories from the Greeks."

"Well, I would hope so." Harriet seemed to feel her point was made. Stretching out her legs still farther, she leaned back and closed her eyes, suggesting, it seemed to Kate, that they both contemplate Demeter.

Kate stared at the ceiling. She could remember reading the story herself in a book on mythology by Edith Hamilton when she was quite young—ten, perhaps, around that. Demeter had an only daughter, Persephone, who had been carried off by the lord of the underworld, carried off significantly, Kate now realized, because she had wandered away from her women companions, as women did yesterday and do still today, enticed yesterday by the beauty of the flower narcissus, today by stories of romance and other accounts of false idylls between men and women. The lord of the underworld, Kate remembered, had risen up through a chasm in the earth and borne Persephone away, weeping, down to his dark dungeon of a kingdom.

But Demeter had power; she controlled the fecundity of the earth, all that grew on it; and to get her daughter back she threatened famine. Nothing grew; nothing could be harvested. Zeus sent emissaries to her; they pleaded with her, trying to turn her from her anger. But Demeter would not let the earth bear fruit until she had again seen her daughter. In the end, Kate remembered, they had made a bargain, which is why there are four or five months of the year when nothing grows. This is the time when Persephone must return to the underworld. But the rest of the year she is with her mother, and the earth once again bears fruit.

"Women no longer have so much power, so much to bargain with," Harriet said after a time, into the silence. "You might say, all I had was you."

"I see," Kate said. "But I will still repeat my question; did you have any children?"

"Yes. We had one child, with whom I'm rather out of touch. We're more than out of touch. We haven't seen each other in years."

"I see," Kate said. It seemed to her that, not inappropriately, she was saying *I see* in every other sentence. "So your main aim wasn't to be a le Carré spy."

"I never said it was. I said I took a hint from le Carré, that's all. To be a le Carré spy, you have to belong to an intelligence service. You have to talk yourself into a dirty frame of mind. You have to think anything you do, any lies you tell, are justified. I am not a le Carré spy, much as I admire George Smiley."

"You seem to feel any lies you tell are justified."

"I resent that, Kate; I deeply resent that. I have told no lies."

"To allow people to draw the wrong conclusion and remain silent, that is to lie."

"It's to spy."

"Well, you have to admit I have a point. It's to use your friends rather than to trust them. True, I might have thought of Demeter. But don't you think Reed would have done exactly the same thing if you had told him the truth?"

"Well, admittedly, I do sometimes suspect that I have a passion for spying. I think we all do, in a way. Spying isn't lying, and that's where spies go wrong. Spying isn't worrying more about your allies than your enemies, which I never did."

"I don't know," Kate said. "If you consider us your allies, you certainly withheld information from us, as you did from your daughter."

"I most certainly did not," Harriet replied hotly. "I can't help it if you didn't catch on; if you've forgotten your Greek myths. I just put a few plots in motion that might help my daughter or might not. I never withheld anything from my daughter in my life. We might have got on better if I had."

"Meaning?"

"Meaning I never liked that man she married, and I liked him even less when he began beating her. She hid it for a long while, but she couldn't hide it forever, even during my infrequent visits. And then when the kids got caught up in it, she really cut me out. I wanted her to leave, you see, and she couldn't quite make up her mind to that. And then, when she shot him, she wouldn't let me see her. She just went limp, she just gave in; I think she really believed they had a right to take the children away from her. I offered to take them, but she wasn't letting me do anything."

"Why not?"

"Who the hell knows why not? Because I opened my big mouth

too often, because of something going far back into her childhood, because she just died to herself for awhile? I had to get her to agree to a defense."

"You may not be Demeter, but you certainly planned the whole thing with great cleverness."

"Believe it or not, the amazing part isn't that I planned the whole thing; I couldn't plan it. I just played the cards as they came along. The amazing thing is that it all worked out. Anyway, don't forget, Kate, that we helped to make that dump into a better law school, we goosed them *and* the students; we accomplished a hell of a lot, if you stop to think of it. You're feeling used, that's your problem; but you weren't used. All I did was get to know you by picking you up at the Theban, after I got the Schuyler job."

"Why did you pick me up? Why did you decide that I could be of use to you?"

"*Of use* is a damn offensive term. I didn't have Demeter's powers. I had damn few powers. In fact, the only power left for women today after they've made a fundamental mistake, is the power to disappear in the old self and reimagine oneself into something, someone, else. That's what I wanted for me and for my daughter. She *was* in the underworld, you know.

"I remembered that Betty had admired you in graduate school," Harriet went on. "I knew that Reed was going to run that clinic. Okay, I persuaded Blair that it would be neat to have Reed's accomplished wife to teach the course with him. I had to hope that Betty might ask for you, that you might reach her as no one else seemed able to do. Damn it to hell, Kate, can't you see that if Reed had agreed to take her case ten times over, he couldn't have done anything if she didn't want him to, and there was no way I could see apart from you to make her want to wake up and decide to face life again. So if that makes me a spy and a criminal and the equal of Karla, who, you will remember, gave up everything for his daughter, I guess I'd better say good-bye, it's been nice knowing you, I'll send you my regards when I see Reed in court."

143

"Sit down," Kate said. "You wanted a drink, you said the day is wearing on, and it's worn on even farther. I'll get us both a drink, and if you try to budge so much as an inch, I'll tackle you."

"I'll only have that drink," Harriet said, "if you promise not to forget Demeter, who had wide dominion. I only had you, and then only on the slimmest of chances. With some hints from George Smiley, of course. Don't you see, Kate, after I got the job at Schuyler—and it was obvious I had to start there, at the place that had condemned her—when, after I got there, I heard that Reed was doing a clinic at prisons, it became obvious that I had to get to you; you were the thread that could lead me through the labyrinth to Betty. To my daughter."

"That's another myth," Kate said.

"Yes, I know. I hope you don't mind being compared to a thread."

"I'm honored," Kate said. "It's humbling of course, being just a thread. Usually, I'm more than that, or convince myself I am. But really, all we detectives do, amateur or professional, even private eyes, even the police, is change the direction of events. None of us really solves anything anymore, do we? We do just try to alter history, however slightly. Now, let me get that drink."

When Kate had returned with the much-admired scotch, when they had both taken a sip, and Harriet had yet again praised the libation, Kate leaned back in her chair and took up the threads of their earlier, more mundane conversation.

"Are you going back to the Boston part of the world?" she asked.

"Only for a visit. I'm staying here. I'm hoping Betty will let me stand by her during the times ahead. Hell, I'm counting on it. Anyway, I'm staying. Do you still want to know me, or is this a farewell drink?"

Kate ignored this. "Are you going to keep up this cash economy business? Are you going to go on being someone without a real identity or your own name?"

"Well, I can't, can I, not if Betty lets me help her. Then I'll be her

mother, so I'll have to have a name, and pay taxes, and be altogether proper and accounted for. And don't say that I cheated the
government, because on Schuyler's generous salary, I always stayed
at the poverty line and didn't owe the government a damn thing."

"And after Betty is released . . ."

"I'm glad you say *after*, not *if*."

"And after Betty is released, will you go back to Boston then?"

"Probably. She may come with me or she may not. That's up to
her. I'll be available when she needs me; she'll know that, and I
hope will think on it. But I have to say that Massachusetts is more
my home than New York, privileged as I have been to know all you
New Yorkers. I'll get some sort of legitimate job, if I don't go to jail
for impersonation and all that rot, and decide on what comes next."

"Well," Kate said, "the next time you take a name, what about
Smiley?"

"What about Fansler? Would you mind if there were two female
Fanslers; you haven't any female relatives of that name, have you?"

"Only three sisters-in-law, and endless nephews and nieces, also
complete with in-laws. I don't think it's advisable."

"You're probably right. The reason I rather like the name Fansler, Kate, is that we are in many ways the same person. Oh, not
superficially, heaven forfend. I don't claim your slimness or your
money or your excellently subdued taste in clothes. But essentially,
we are the same—in spirit, you might say. I am what you may be in
time, if you play your cards right."

"I won't have a daughter."

"Not biologically, no. I can't say I think a lot of the usual mother-
daughter connection. We may work it out someday; we haven't so
far, not in most cases. But you'll have an honorary daughter or two,
I hope not in prison, but somewhere, needing you just to exist and
encourage."

"You're a bloody romantic, Harriet. But I guess I already knew
that. Only I called you a spy instead."

"I'm not a romantic, damn it," Harriet said, "but speaking of romantics, don't think I didn't see you giving our Blair the once-over—he's cute, I'll admit that. But for you and me, we knew that none of that's to do with life, really. Sex is fine if you want it, if you have it, if you do it right. But it's not what I was ever all about, and it's certainly not what I'm all about now, and that means I'm not a bloody romantic. Do you know what le Carré said about Smiley on the subject?"

"Oh, God, how I wish I did remember, and could quote it to you on the spot." Just as I wish I'd remembered Demeter, Kate thought.

"Well, you can't, so I'll tell you. He said: 'Each morning as he got out of bed, each evening as he went back to it, usually alone, he had reminded himself that he never was and never had been indispensable.' Well, maybe not. But he and you and I are more indispensable than most people, and don't you forget it."

"I can never forget you, or Smiley either, for that matter," Kate said, "and I shall feel a surge of pleasure when I think of either of you. And you're wrong about Blair."

"No I'm not, but you're too intelligent to launch into *that*, and too aware of the value of what you've got."

"So now you're a marriage counselor." Kate laughed.

"Chuckle on. When Betty's habeas is over, I'll be gone from your life; but as age creeps on, as you say to yourself, is this all there is? What the hell is this crazy time? Well, when that happens, you think of me. Not how I look, or exactly how I acted, but how I did things, how I made things happen, how I risked a lot for what I decided needed to be done, how I remembered Demeter, above all, how I helped to change and even maybe transform one moldy institution. Somewhere in your psyche you'll be worrying about growing old. Think of me, and remember that it's fun."

"Okay," Kate said. "I'll try to remember, when all is wrinkles and liver spots and ubiquitous sagging. Meanwhile all I have to say to you is that you're not Demeter, you're a witch, you're not a spy, either, although you may have made spies of the rest of us, you're a witch and I think you had better climb onto your broomstick and fly away."

"Not till I've had another shot of that single-malt scotch," Harriet said, holding out her glass.

❦❦Epilogue

I do find I become a great deal more radical in my old age.

—JOHN LE CARRÉ
THE SECRET PILGRIM

And at last the semester ended.

"Would you like to have one last dinner at the Oak Room, to celebrate the successful conclusion of our course and our institutional revolution?" Blair asked Kate as she was finally clearing out all her belongings from his office.

She paused a moment, holding her purse and briefcase, with her jacket over her arm. "Thank you for asking," she said. "That was nice of you. But I think I'll just go home and try to sneak back into my old self. Not all of my old self, actually, but the part that just teaches literature to people who signed up to learn it, not to lawyers."

"It's no use trying to fool yourself or lull yourself, you know," Blair said. "Not that I'm urging you to have dinner with me, however pleasant that would be. I understand about dinner. But do try to bear in mind that we live in new and frightening times. We live with corporate rot and a total loss of purpose, whether we mean nationally, internationally, or in institutions. That's why extreme right-wingers succeed, if they come along when the rest of us are closing our eyes, going on with what we usually, comfortably do, and waiting for something nice to happen. Sorry," he added. "I didn't know I was going to make a speech."

"You're right," Kate said. "You must come and teach law and literature on my turf sometime; I think that's an excellent idea. But I don't think I care for spying, if that's what I was doing. That's what Harriet would call it. Well, spy or not, I feel as though I got pushed into a fight I hadn't meant to be in."

"We can only fight the wars we inherit, whether we're nations or individuals," Blair said. "We inherited this fight, and we fought it—honorably, I think. Don't delude yourself you're too good for such fights; that's a liberal delusion that has devoured our causes, if I'm allowed to assume we have the same causes."

"Well, you saw the danger and took on the fight and I think you deserve a lot of credit. But I shall never be able to square with myself the thought of being a spy."

"That's nonsense," Blair said. "Think back, my dear; think back. We all become spies as children; that's the only way we know to make sense of the world."

Harriet said much the same thing when she came sometime later for a farewell drink with Kate and Reed.

"We learn from childhood to take refuge in secrecy," she said. "How else could we survive? And it's very easy to translate that into spying."

"Perhaps," Kate said. "But I still have a sense of having come to Schuyler as a spy, or at least under false pretenses—saying I would teach law and literature, not foment a revolution."

"But it wasn't false pretenses," Harriet insisted. "You told the school exactly what you were going to do. And you did it. What's spying about that?"

"We hoped the students would wake up and do something to change the school."

"Isn't that what teaching always is, or should be? Hoping the students will wake up and question their surroundings and the conditions they live in? I can't see what's spying about that."

"Well, what about Reed, then?"

"Reed was doing exactly what he said he would do—operating

the first real clinic at Schuyler Law," Harriet said. "In this case, helping prisoners to appeal. No false pretenses."

Reed smiled at her. "On the face of it, no false pretenses," he said. "I agreed to do a clinic and I did it. But I had my reasons, unknown to Schuyler Law. I wanted to shake myself up a bit and please Kate. Yes, I'm convinced of the merit of the clinic I ran; I hope it continues running without me there. But I had my secret aims, and I, too, ended up changing the Schuyler Law School. Hardly all clear and beyond suspicion."

"You're all disenchanted romantics," Harriet said, chuckling. "You all have a great hunger for goodness. You saw a chance to correct a wrong, and you took it. That's not what spies do, not according to le Carré or anyone else. I think you are both trying to make yourselves out to be moles. Hell, we all have agendas, we all have hopes for change; but you didn't lie to anyone, you and Kate. You didn't even keep secrets from each other, which proves you're not spies, if anything could."

"Didn't we?" Kate asked.

"No," Reed said. "We didn't. And in a way, Harriet's right. Without us, they would have gone on. It's not that we *did* anything dramatic. We just frightened them as a result of being there. We didn't infiltrate; we were ourselves. Spies infiltrate."

"To be a le Carré spy," Harriet announced firmly, "you have to belong to a government agency, probably secret and certainly lying to the public and everybody else. You have to talk yourself into a dirty frame of mind. You have to think anything you do, any lies you tell, are justified. I'd say you're all exonerated; you're not spies."

"But you are," Kate said. "You lied about your connection to Reed's client. Well, you lied by silence, which is the worst kind. You lied to me when we met, or damn near. I don't think you get off not being a spy."

"Okay. As I said so often, I'm like Smiley. I have a trained, observant mind. I notice things. I have his guarded, watchful way of looking at the world. But, unlike him, I'm not in a secret service, so I haven't lost my center, which he damn near did."

"But he turned up with different names, claiming to be different people, not admitting to being himself," Kate argued, not that she knew why. A warm contentment had come over her, the sort you sometimes get at a certain point in an illness, when you feel cared for and somehow safe.

"Of course," Harriet said, ignoring this, "I might be said to have been on a mission of vengeance, as Smiley was, against Karla. But it wasn't really vengeance, it was rescue. You know, at the end, when Smiley has caught Karla, saved him, really, him and his daughter, given Karla a chance to be someone else, Peter Guillam says to Smiley, 'You won,' and Smiley says, 'Did I? Yes, I guess I did.' Well, I guess I did; I won. Betty's going to have another chance."

"Let's drink to that," Reed said.

So, in the end, Harriet flew back to Boston. She went coach this time, and the man sitting next to her paid no attention to her or her book, which was, of course, the latest novel by her favorite author, a gift from Kate. He's carrying on without the secret service, she told herself, so I guess we all can.

The truth was that Harriet had discovered a great desire in herself to fight deception, and intolerance, and bigotry, and as she readily recognized, hers was a desire not easily slaked or ignored. Damn those bastards anyway and all who sail with them, she said to herself. The man next to her, seeing her smile, smiled back.

AMANDA CROSS is the pseudonymous author of the popular Kate Fansler mysteries, of which *An Imperfect Spy* is the eleventh.

As Carolyn G. Heilbrun, she is the Avalon Foundation Professor in the Humanities Emerita at Columbia University, and the author of *Writing a Woman's Life* and other works of literary criticism.